THE BRIDE'S TRAIL

by A.A. Abbott

Published by Perfect City Press.

ISBN 978-0-9929621-1-1

A WORD FROM THE AUTHOR

Thanks to my team, especially Donna Marie Finn, David Massey, and lovely librarian Jackie Molloy, who volunteered for a cameo role.

A.A. Abbott

BY AA ABBOTT

Up In Smoke

After The Interview

The Bride's Trail

*See **http://aaabbott.co.uk** for my blog, free short stories and more*

*Follow AA Abbott on Twitter **@AAAbbottStories** and on **Facebook***

Contents

Chapter 1 Amy

"Had a hairspray fire today," Kat reported. As usual, she was wired on her return from work.

"Really?" Amy turned on the tap, splashed water into a glass. London's summer heat had settled into every corner of their basement flat. The air was stifling. She yawned, fragments of dreams still clouding her head. Slamming the front door at three in the morning, Kat had only half-woken her.

"January, the new croupier," Kat continued. "She'd just done her hair, then she lit a cigarette. We're not supposed to smoke in the loo, but we all do." Kat tutted. "Then, boom!"

"Is she okay?"

"Needs a haircut." Kat laughed. "She needed one before, anyhow. Wearing a ponytail to one side is wrong on every level past the age of twelve."

"How old is she?" Amy's curiosity overcame her drowsiness. Kat always made the casino sound so glamorous, and it paid well, although not enough to fund Kat's designer dress habit.

"Says she's twenty one. If you ask me, going on thirty." Kat yawned. "Must sleep. I'm getting married in the morning."

"Who to? Jeb?" It was the first name that sprang to mind, although he was the last man that Amy herself would choose for a mate. There was a hint of evil about him, a calculating gaze that chilled her. Even his roguish smile, smooth coffee-coloured skin and abundant charm couldn't compensate for that. What was he to Kat, exactly? Once, she'd called him a gangster. She'd always denied he was her boyfriend. He never stayed the night. Despite that, Kat often disappeared with him to the nightspots in Charlotte Street. Only round the corner, it was a honeypot for both of them. Just north of London's Oxford Street, Fitzrovia had all the party potential of Soho to the south, without its sleaze.

Amy frowned. The lack of a wedding invitation, or even a wine-fuelled chat about the occasion, was a little hurtful. After two months sharing a flat, she would have expected to go to the party.

"Too many questions, my dear!" Kat laughed. "Definitely not Jeb. He isn't rich enough. An Asian guy, Bangladeshi. He's not rich either, but it's only a short-term arrangement. Please be a darling, Amy. Can you knock on my bedroom door tomorrow morning? Just in case I don't wake up early."

There was no need, though. When the shrill siren of her alarm drove her out of bed at seven, Amy could already hear Kat moving around.

"Want to see my dress?" Kat asked, peeping out from her bedroom into the lobby that also served as a kitchen.

The flat was cramped. When the 1970s apartment block had been built forty years earlier, these basement rooms had been a storage area. The subsequent conversion was optimistic. Technically, it was a one bedroom property. The bedroom, however, barely had space for a single bed. Kat had sublet it to Amy and commandeered the lounge for herself. Although a larger room, there was nowhere to fit an ironing board. Kat's white frock was laid out on a small dining table covered with towels.

"What do you think?" Kat asked, steaming iron in hand.

The low-cut silk and lace confection flowed like a foamy waterfall over the table's edge. It would look stunning on Kat's curves, not to mention offsetting her creamy skin and long blonde hair. "Wow," Amy said.

"It's a Stella," Kat said, omitting to mention the designer's surname. There was really no need. "Too good for Ahmed, but I'll use it again. By the way, I forgot to tell you – Ross visited the casino last night. He was very chatty, actually."

"Who's Ross?"

"You know, the stud who lives in the penthouse flat upstairs. Bronwen, my last flatmate, had a crush on him. You can see him in the gym next door sometimes." While most of the basement was occupied by a car park, next to their flat was a small room crammed with fitness equipment. The girls sometimes heard the hum of the treadmill through their thin partition walls.

"Oh, him," Amy said dismissively. "He works at Veritable Insurance, so he'll be as boring as the rest of them."

"Yes, he told me he was an actuary. But if everyone who works there is boring, what does that say about you?" Kat teased, her green eyes merry.

"I don't belong there. It's just a stepping stone," Amy pointed out. The sole redeeming feature of her workplace was the monthly salary it paid every month. Even that was poor; it vanished quickly. "Anyway, what do you fancy most about Ross: the size of his wallet or the size of his muscles?"

Kat winked.

As she left the flat, Amy heard clattering in the gym and realised the step machine was in use. She peeked through the glass door. She recognised Ross immediately: a young man with curly, fair hair and the physique of a Greek god. He would be handsome if he didn't look so pleased with himself.

Ross glanced up. His deep blue eyes met hers, showed total indifference and promptly looked away again. Amy was discomfited. While she wasn't attracted to Ross in the least, she would have liked some appreciation of her appearance. As usual, she'd made an effort for work: her hair was straightened, shirt pressed, make-up fresh.

Amy walked briskly in her trainers, mulling over the ways of men. She couldn't pretend to understand them. Her parents had always assured her she was beautiful, and all around there was evidence that slimness was alluring. Indeed, towering over her friends as a teenager and skinnier than anyone she knew, she'd dreamed of being a supermodel. All the glossy magazines Kat bought had pictures of girls like Amy, beanpoles with inscrutable, some might even say grumpy, expressions. Yet men stayed away, flocking instead to Kat's fuller figure.

It wasn't far from Fitzrovia to the City, and it was a pleasant walk. The air had cooled at last, morning sun just burning through cloud before the streets overheated later in the day. The attractive jumble of tall, flat-fronted brick houses and sixties office blocks that Amy loved in Fitzrovia gave way to more offices and shops as she passed the souvenir emporiums of Oxford Street. Her route became busier, with traffic and pedestrians rushing past the Centre Point skyscraper and down the thriving thoroughfare of Charing Cross Road. She watched street sweepers clean evidence of night-time revels as she crossed Trafalgar Square, finally striding along the Embankment and enjoying a view of the languid river before reaching Veritable's office. This was a huge, unlovely, concrete cuboid in the shadow of Blackfriars Bridge. Amy made it in thirty minutes, saving the Tube fare. She changed into court shoes on arrival. They were a shiny plastic that was supposed to look like leather, and all she could afford since her credit card maxed out.

"Good morning, Parveen." Annoyingly, Parveen was already there, so relaxing with Facebook was out of the question.

Amy's boss glanced at the clock on the wall. "Eight o'clock meeting, Amy."

"Oh. I didn't know. Anyway, it's ten to."

"You should read your emails. And we need a pre-meeting first." Parveen raised her eyes to the ceiling. "Do you have those mood boards ready?"

She had forgotten. Parveen realised it before Amy could say anything. "You put it off, right? Because it was difficult. Well, I'll reschedule the meeting with Bert. Just get them done, OK? Start now. What am I always telling you? Swallow a live frog before breakfast."

That was Parveen's mantra. Do the difficult stuff first. Of course, as a manager, Parveen must have very little to do herself. That was obvious from the way she immediately phoned Bert, batting her eyelashes as she explained that David Saxton had given her team a special project, so the product literature just had to wait a couple of days, and could she buy him lunch to say sorry?

It was evident from Parveen's body language that Bert had fallen for her wheedling tone, even if he couldn't see her soulful eyes and long lashes.

"What's the project?" Amy asked as Parveen replaced her phone.

"There isn't one," Parveen said scornfully. "As if David Saxton knows who we are – we're too far down the food chain for that, and so's Bert. He'll never find out. Hurry up with that frog."

It wasn't just one frog, Amy reflected sourly, but many. As Parveen sent an intern to collect coffees and wrote emails ordering the rest of the team to tackle the labours of Hercules, Amy began her task. She'd imagined her marketing degree would lead to a job in fashion, or a high tech company where she could hang out with hip young engineers. Veritable Insurance meant wearing a suit, spending long days with other people who wore suits and seemed to like it, and scouring the internet for images and phrases that would sell household insurance.

"Are you on Facebook?" Parveen asked sharply.

"No." Amy's face flamed. "Just surfing for stock images. How do you like 'Safe as houses', by the way."

Parveen shrugged her shoulders. "It's a cliché. You can do better than that."

Amy was distracted by a glimpse of Ross strolling towards them, his gym wear replaced by a dark suit and crisp shirt. He was wearing spectacles, an achingly trendy pair with thick black frames. They didn't spoil his looks at all, simply giving him the air of an intellectual.

As an actuary, his spot in the open plan office was many yards away, close to the glass-fronted meeting rooms that overlooked the Thames. Like a despised poor relation, the marketing department languished in a dark corner, deprived of the sunlight blazing down on the City. Amy waved, about to declare it was an honour to be graced with a visit.

Ross blanked her even more effectively than he'd done a few hours before, walking straight past without so much as a glance. Were his spectacles made of plain glass, purely worn for effect? They certainly hadn't helped him notice her. As Parveen glared, Amy saw Ross stop at the coffee machine. She was suddenly reminded of her broken night. Caffeine was exactly what she needed too.

Chapter 2 Ross

Ross noticed the dreary girl waving at him, and realised with a start that he'd seen her already this morning. She had walked past the gym. Presumably she lived in the poky little flat next to it, although it would be a stretch on her salary; he had seen it advertised at £1,500 a month. He hoped she was his neighbour, because otherwise, she must be stalking him. He shuddered at the thought. Tall, flat-chested redheads would never be his type. Shapely green-eyed blondes were a different matter. He must return to the Diamonds casino soon, see Kat again and ask her out. She'd really appreciated being offered champagne last night, although she'd said sorrowfully that she wasn't allowed to drink at work. They had chatted for a while, though, about mathematics and probability and cards. It was refreshing to meet a woman who understood him, especially such a stunner.

It had been a lucky night. Ross had only visited Diamonds because a group of friends were going. While he regularly supplemented his salary with online poker winnings, he hadn't expected to make money at the casino. Chance was against him, as he had explained to the attentive Kat. To his surprise, he had pocketed several hundred pounds during the evening, as well as enjoying a free bar. He grinned to himself. He would definitely be back.

It was annoying that the coffee machine next to his desk was out of order, all the more because the dreary girl had decided to join him at this one.

"Hi," she said.

He gritted his teeth. "Hi."

"I'm Amy from Marketing," she said, extending a hand.

He didn't take it. "Ross," he said, curtly.

"Where do you work, Ross?"

He gazed around the open plan area. "What do you think? I'm here at Veritable, like you."

"I mean, which function?" She seemed to be sensing his reluctance, because she said, "Oh, I remember. You're an actuary. Kat told me."

He stared at her, open-mouthed, flattered that Kat would talk about him but wondering why she'd chosen to do so with Amy. "How do you know her?" he asked.

"She's my flatmate," Amy said.

Ross laughed. In an effort to hide his excitement, he remarked, "Two of you? There's barely room to swing a kitten in there." He recalled visiting the small basement flat when a caretaker had lived there, before the freeholder for the block realised how much money could be made by renting it out. If Amy shared the flat, that explained how she could afford to rent in Fitzrovia. Even so, she might have a trust fund, or rich parents. He'd heard rumours that the CEO had given a junior marketing job to a young relative. Perhaps it was her.

Ross could imagine himself as CEO one day. Like David Saxton, he would be a commanding presence, strolling through the office as if he owned it, driving a Jag, giving interviews to the Financial Times. "I hear Davey Saxton has a niece in the marketing department," he said to Amy.

She shrugged. Maybe it wasn't true, then. It certainly couldn't be her. Her voice had a common edge, betraying state school origins in London, or more likely a dull dormitory town nearby. Saxton's family would doubtless send their offspring to be privately educated, as Ross had been himself. He opened the small fridge next to the coffee machine and made a pretence of looking for milk, so he no longer needed to make eye contact with Amy and she would see their conversation was at an end.

Chapter 3 Shaun

The day had started well for Shaun. He'd visited the old factory unit in Tottenham, and found the builders had nearly finished. They were excessively polite and he caught a couple of sharp glances from them. Jeb had obviously been round to motivate the lads. Whether Jeb had roughed them up or merely threatened it, he neither knew nor cared.

His sons were still in bed when he arrived home in Wanstead. Shaun shook the older one awake. "Time you were up and doing something useful," he said.

"I went to bed late." Ben's tone was injured innocence. "I've been practicing for the gaming tournament."

"Why can't you use that computer productively?" Shaun felt his cheeks flush, his fists clench. At Ben's age, he had done over a hundred burglaries. At least, that was the number to which he'd admitted the first and only time he was sentenced. "Clone some credit cards, hack into a bank, or," he racked his brains, "close down one of those shopping sites your mum liked, and hold them to ransom." He wished he knew the first thing about cyber-crime such as this; he was simply aware that younger men were doing well from it. Men in their early thirties; Jeb's age, but with more brains. Shaun remained surprised when Jeb, perhaps by pointing to a newspaper or programming a satnav, revealed that he could read.

"Meh," Ben said, yawning. For an aching, fleeting moment, he looked like Meg.

Shaun's anger dissipated. He harrumphed and retreated downstairs to heat a ready meal. Meg had wanted the boys to study, to go to university, a novel concept for Shaun but one that he was prepared to entertain for his wife's sake. She usually had her way, and she was always proved right. At least, Ben had spent a shiny-eyed year at London Metropolitan, rising early, reading books and using his laptop to pursue interests other than video games. It had all gone wrong three years ago, with Meg's death from cancer. Everything had gone wrong, except his business. He had poured all his energy into it, neglecting his sons but numbing his grief.

Buying and selling was the secret of his success. His father had been an expert burglar and had taught Shaun everything he knew, but Shaun always had wider ambitions. As thieves, you were at the mercy of the middleman who bought from you. Far better to be that middleman yourself, taking a commission here and a profit there, dealing in drugs, stolen goods, bodies; anything that could be sold. Shaun shook his head. Thanks to eBay and car boot sales, he now believed there was nothing that couldn't be sold. Everything had a price; everybody too, come to that.

He had thrown himself into work after Meg's death. Despite the aching loss, he still had the golden touch. Jeb, his right-hand man, was an efficient enforcer. Shaun also relied heavily on a bent accountant, a man expert at laundering his ill-gotten gains and keeping the taxman at bay. The Tottenham venture was bound to be a success.

He needed to stop worrying about his sons and relax. An evening at Diamonds was just the ticket. Jeb knew a girl there, didn't he, a potential employee for Tottenham? The two of them should make a night out of it.

Just as Shaun thought, Jeb was up for a night in the West End. Gambling had always been Jeb's weakness. The younger man had even sought counselling in his prison days. It must have been serious; Jeb indulged freely in booze, cigarettes and cocaine without complaining of addiction. He must be backsliding. Shaun resolved to watch him like a hawk.

Shaun dressed with care, choosing an Armani summer suit, cut from off-white linen. An East End boy, he would hold his own in the West End. As he knotted his white silk tie, he frowned at his reflection: the greying hair and jowls that had appeared as he hurtled towards fifty. His bright blue shirt flattered him though, bringing out the colour of his eyes and skimming over his paunch to give an illusion of

18

slenderness. Meg had bought it for him. His mirror-polished shoes, by contrast, he had ordered himself from a cobbler who made them by hand. They added an inch to his height. While he could never be as tall as Jeb, he at least appeared above average.

Jeb, arriving in Wanstead in a BMW with rap blaring from the stereo, was darkly handsome in a charcoal suit. A sheen of oil glistened on his short, black curls. Now he'd removed the single gold earring and nose ring he usually wore, he looked like an estate agent or kitchen salesman. He stared at Shaun with evident disbelief. "This isn't a Saturday Night Fever convention," he muttered.

Shaun put Jeb right with a few choice words. "Slip a tenner to the doorman, you can get in anywhere," he finished, sage advice that his father had given him and which turned out to be true that evening.

Shaun had visited Diamonds several times before and was gratified that the staff remembered his preferences. He was ushered to the roulette wheel and asked if he would like to book a table for dinner, perhaps to have some well-hung fillet steak. Jeb trailed after him, his usual swagger as subdued as his clothing. The fibres of his suit caught the light, a tell-tale sign that it had cost less than a tenth of Shaun's Armani threads.

"I'll put a hundred on red," Shaun said, and the evening began.

Shaun knew very well that the odds favoured the house; it was why he believed gambling was a business opportunity. Simply betting on red, he won on a few spins of the wheel, lost on a few more and almost broke even. Jeb, on the other hand, made arcane bets on combinations of numbers, losing nearly a thousand pounds. He seemed unfocused, reckless as he threw the chips down. Perspiration beaded his face.

Shaun took him to one side. "You've been at the Charlie," he hissed. He peered into Jeb's eyes. Despite the inviting glow of the low lights over the gaming tables, it was too dark to tell.

"I never touch it," Jeb protested, unconvincingly.

"What's with these stupid bets, then? You can't afford it," Shaun whispered.

19

"What? It's hot in here, isn't it?" Jeb said, mopping his brow. "I'll have to go outside for a smoke."

It was possible Jeb's cheap suit was the problem. Shaun doubted it. He was sure Jeb had overdone the powder. "I'll come with you. Listen, we'll leave after we've eaten, OK?" he suggested. "Just introduce me to that girl you mentioned. You said she'd do some work for me."

"You mean Kat? She's over there," Jeb said, pointing to a horseshoe-shaped blackjack table.

Shaun stared at the blonde laughing and joking with a bunch of city suits as she handed over their winnings. She exuded charisma and he was surprised he hadn't noticed her before. Still, blackjack was not his game of choice. It was one for professionals, or city boys who thought they could beat the house.

The blackjack players couldn't keep their eyes off her. Of course, she was at the centre of the horseshoe, and she was pretty, her tied-back curls reminiscent of Marilyn Monroe. Her uniform, a crisp white shirt, black waistcoat and miniskirt, suited her figure. It was more than that, though. As Kat caught his eye and smiled, he realised it was her self-assurance that attracted men. Like addicts seeking a hit, they clustered around her.

Kat waved to Jeb. "I'll be on my break in ten minutes," she mouthed, before turning to the suits and beginning to deal once more.

The casino had a patio for smokers. Shaun fished around in his pocket, retrieving his cigarettes. He offered them to Jeb, who accepted gratefully. After a couple of deep drags, Jeb regained his composure. He had a smile ready for Kat when she joined them. "Hi Kat. Want a light?" Jeb flicked a flame out of his lighter, a flashy gold number with a skull and crossbones picked out in sparkly stones.

"No, thanks," Kat shook her head almost imperceptibly. She had the grace of a unicorn. "We're not allowed to smoke at work. You should know that, Jeb."

"Rules are made to be broken," Jeb said.

"How do you cope?" Shaun asked, curious. "I'd be gasping for one inside the hour."

"I guess I'm a social smoker," Kat replied. Her eyes, jade-green, looked into Shaun's for the first time. "We haven't been introduced." She held out her hand.

Shaun shook it firmly. "I'm Shaun."

"Shaun's my boss," Jeb said. "I know you like your dresses, Kat. Shaun has a proposition for you that'll help you pay those credit card bills." He stumbled over the sentence; proposition was a long word for him.

Shaun imagined Kat in a low-cut dress, then wearing even less. He chided himself. She didn't look that type and she had a posh voice. "How would you like to earn some extra money, Kat? Cash in hand."

Kat laughed throatily, a pleasant sound that reminded him of jazz singers. "I'm open to opportunities," she said. "What did you have in mind?"

"I need a croupier for a new casino – an unofficial one." He stopped there, giving her time to digest his words.

Kat cottoned on quickly. "You mean a speakeasy?" she asked, her smile dazzling him.

"Yes, a speakeasy," Shaun said. "I like that word." It conjured up visions of prohibition, of gravel-voiced gamblers drinking cocktails in smoke-filled bars. He resolved to employ a mixologist as well.

"Where is it?" Kat asked. "I live in Fitzrovia; I don't travel south of the river."

"No worries," Jeb said. "It's in Tottenham."

Shaun wished Jeb had kept quiet. Kat's smile blazed less brightly. Tottenham was always going to be a difficult sell to someone like her, a classy girl living in the West End. "It has to be off the beaten track," he said. "It's exclusive, a secret destination. Those in the know will travel there specially. You don't have to walk through the neighbourhood. I'll pay for taxis, door to door."

"I'll give you a lift, Kat," Jeb said.

21

"There's no need," Kat said, with a wry glance. "What kind of custom are you expecting?" she asked, turning her gaze towards Shaun's again.

Usually, he could read people's eyes, yet Shaun realised hers were telling him nothing. Her expression was friendly, but entirely business-like. She gave away no emotion: no enthusiasm, desire or disdain. He respected her for it. "Entrepreneurs like myself," Shaun replied. "Gentlemen and ladies who want to enjoy themselves without the government telling them what to do."

"He means smokers," Jeb said. "And people who like a drink."

Shaun's lips pursed. "We're not talking crusties drinking strong lager and coughing over roll-ups," he said. "I'm not chasing the losers who play on one-armed bandits."

"Quite right too," Jeb agreed. "Those guys cause trouble. Although nothing I can't handle, if I say so myself."

Kat giggled. "You sound like a gangster, Jeb."

"Is that so?" Jeb said with mock irony. He winked at Shaun.

"I want the sort of punters who come here." Shaun scanned the patio, noting several smokers whose clothing and languages were foreign, and caveated his words. "Actually, a British customer base. No Chinese, Sheikhs, oligarchs or Poles. Londoners with money to spend in a relaxed environment. They can have a bit of a flutter, drink cocktails, try a cigar – all premium imported brands, of course."

"Like Snow Mountain vodka?" Kat asked, to his surprise.

"Yes, high end brands like that. Why Snow Mountain in particular?"

She shrugged her shoulders, a movement that, from anyone else, might speak of contempt. When Kat did it, it was simply elegant. "I was always told it was the best," she said.

"I'll make sure to get it," Shaun said. Why not? He would send a white van over to Belgium to bring back anything he needed. The warehouses over there stocked every brand under the sun, at bargain prices because their tax was lower. He allowed himself a moment of self-righteous indignation at the criminal level of taxation imposed by the British government. It was practically an entrepreneur's duty to evade it.

Kat stretched and yawned in a fluid movement, reminding Shaun of a ballet dancer. "Excuse me," she said. "My break's nearly over and I have to powder my nose."

"Oh yes?" Jeb winked.

"Not the way you do," she retorted.

"Wait," Shaun said. He had expected more time to discuss his beloved project with her. "Are you interested?"

"In working for you?" Kat asked. "You want croupiers, don't you? I'd love to help, but I'm not looking for another job. I've only been working here for a month."

"You need some extra money, Kat," Jeb wheedled, his voice soft as marshmallows and sweet as honey. "They don't pay what you're worth in this place, and your designer clothes don't come cheap. You could work a couple of shifts for Shaun, surely?" He touched her arm lightly.

It was enough to stop her walking away. "You need more than one croupier twice a week," Kat said. "How about you bring in some girls and I'll train them? I'm sure Jeb has friends he can send along."

Shaun eyed her with admiration. Kat clearly had Jeb's measure. She had subtly mentioned his cocaine habit, and his women. Better still, Jeb hadn't noticed. "Of course," he said. "Forty pounds an hour, cash."

"Sixty," Kat said. "Sequentially numbered notes; no forgeries."

"Agreed," Shaun said, offering a handshake. "Write down your phone number and I'll be in touch to agree a start date."

He joined Jeb in staring at Kat's bottom as she walked away.

"Nice arse," Jeb said.

"You're not wrong," Shaun agreed. "You haven't had her, have you?"

Jeb inhaled on his cigarette, looking up at the sky.

"I know I'm right." Shaun said.

"Any day now," Jeb said, exhaling a blue cloud.

"You're offering her plenty of the white powder, I suppose?" Shaun said. "To ease her knickers off?"

Jeb grinned.

"You're wasting your time," Shaun said. "She won't take it from you." Sure, it had worked for Jeb before; many times. He had a string of girls right now, ready to service him and anyone else who paid for the pleasure. Kat was different from the others, though. Her accent put her in a stratospheric social class compared with them. Shaun was surprised she had the time of day for Jeb. He couldn't see that Jeb had anything to offer her.

"She will," Jeb protested. "Kat's got an addictive personality. She smokes, right?"

"You heard the lady. She's a social smoker. And," Shaun glared, "she's not a rough slag. She's a posh bird. They operate by different rules. Plus I need her to train my croupiers, so back off."

"You dirty dog. You want her for yourself." Jeb's lip curled, then he smiled, appearing suddenly to remember who was boss.

Was Jeb right? Shaun imagined fondling Kat's bottom and squeezing her firm breasts. He shook his head. Since Meg died, womanising was no fun, not even the droit de seigneur he enjoyed over Jeb's harem of young blonde addicts. He wished he knew why. Anyway, while he rated Jeb's chances with Kat as slim to none, his own were even lower.

Chapter 4   Charles

"You must meet Mark," Deirdre said, flicking her expensively toffee-coloured locks away from her face.

Charles fixed a grin on his face, while groaning inside. He had been about to step outside for a cigarette. Clearly, the five minutes Deirdre had spent speaking to Mark, a small, bald man, was enough for her. She wanted to circulate and would be expecting Charles to divert Mark's attention.

"My partner, Chas," Deirdre said to Mark. "He works in banking."

"I suppose we've got you to blame for the financial crisis, then," Mark said. "Ha ha ha."

"Ha ha ha," echoed Charles, feeling, as always when the subject arose, that this was rather unfair. He doubted the world's finances had been hit when his team persuaded two antiquated computer systems to talk to each other. He knew better than to explain the finer points of IT to Deirdre and her chums, though. She'd warned him such expositions were tedious.

"So you're the lucky man," Mark said, ogling Deirdre as she sparkled among a group of middle-aged women in jewel-bright cocktail dresses. "She looks like the cat with the cream. Many of us had hopes, but alas..."

"Yes," Charles replied. He felt insulted that Mark would regard himself as competition: the small man's girth almost matched his height, producing the effect of a shiny-topped cube. Charles was quietly proud of making it to his mid-forties without hair loss or middle-aged spread. What on earth should he say next? "I don't suppose you've got a light?" he ventured.

"Yes, actually," Mark replied. "I'm surprised Dee allows you to smoke. Thought a woman like her would be wearing the trousers."

"That's where you're wrong," Charles said. "This may be her flat and her friends, but I'm here because I choose to be." Even as he said them, he wasn't quite convinced by his own words. He would much rather be at Deirdre's drinks party than staying late at work, however, and he knew a cigarette would improve his mood. "Let's go outside."

They stood on the balcony overlooking the Mayfair square's gardens. A solitary worker was tending a lawn that already looked green, neat and trim as a snooker table. "Ah, you're a Marlboro man," Mark said. "Me too. I hate these networking events, by the way; can only get through them with whisky and cigarettes."

"Why do you turn up, then?" Charles asked, his curiosity piqued. His own presence was easy to explain: it was required by Deirdre. He, too, used nicotine to alleviate the stress and boredom of meeting strangers with whom he had nothing in common.

Mark looked back over his shoulder. "Dee's such a good connector," he said. "When she hosts a gathering, she makes sure you meet people who can help you in your business."

"What's your line of work?" Charles asked.

"Similar to Dee," Mark replied.

"Fitness?" Charles nearly choked on his cigarette. An awful vision of Mark clad only in shorts and trainers swam into his mind. Mark's physique was not so much pillowy as a whole duvet of flesh wrapped around his body.

"No, videos," Mark said. "I shoot and stream them online for a subscription, like Dee does with her fitness classes."

Charles imagined porn movies in which cube-shaped Mark was the star. He began to feel nauseous, and drew on his cigarette for comfort. "Yes," he said, his tone non-committal.

"I do corporate work as well," Mark continued. "Today, I had a marketing shoot for Veritable Insurance." He lowered his voice. "Between you and me, I wouldn't work with them again for double the money. Terrible. There was a dreadfully rude woman called Parveen who kept panicking and interrupting the shots."

"My daughter works for her," Charles said, thankful that Mark's work was nowhere near as interesting as he'd feared. Amy had bent his ear about a manager called Parveen. It had to be the same person.

"She has my sympathy," Mark snorted. "I'd find another job if I were her."

"She struggled to get that one. Dee had to pull strings. Her brother's the CEO there." Charles remembered not to use his partner's given name; she regarded it as ageing.

"Really?" Mark whistled. "I know she lives in this fabulous flat, but I didn't think Dee was born with a silver spoon in her mouth."

"She wasn't," Charles said. "We knew each other at school. She used to smoke then."

He recalled Deirdre, nervous and chubby, lighting a cigarette for the first time. He'd been skulking with a couple of friends in the school's old and overgrown air raid shelter, known as Smokers' Corner. The bike shed was too heavily policed. His best friend, Tim, had brought a magazine adorned with pictures of naked women. All three fifteen-year-olds were poring over it.

"I say, have any of you chaps got a light?"

The boys turned round. Tim hastily stuffed the magazine in his school bag.

"Well, look who it is! Davey Saxton's sister." Richard, like the others, was in the school football team. They all knew Davey, a curly-haired twelve-year-old who showed great promise on the soccer field. His sister, her hair mousy and windswept, looked every inch as sporty. She was wearing trainers, a cotton top and shorts. The outfit did nothing for her chunky thighs, although it revealed a bounteous bosom.

"What's your name, Davey Saxton's sister?" Charles asked, making no attempt to look any higher than her cleavage.

"Deirdre. I'm his older sister." Her answer revealed teeth imprisoned behind braces. She added, in response to their cynical expressions, "I'm fourteen."

27

"I happen to have some matches," Charles said. She would have deduced that. All three boys were puffing at cancer sticks, which they must have ignited somehow.

Deirdre grinned awkwardly, and asked, "Can you light it for me?"

"Crumbs," Richard said with contempt, "it's your first one, isn't it?"

She giggled with embarrassment.

"There's a first time for everything," Charles said, rather smoothly, he felt. "What you have to do is breathe in as soon as I light it, okay? Where are your cigarettes, anyway?"

Deirdre reached into her shorts pocket, producing a cellophane-wrapped packet of Dunhill.

Richard goggled at them. "Did you pinch them from your Dad?" he sniggered. None of them could afford the pricier brands. They sometimes bought singles from the local Indian shop, or clubbed together for the cheapest packet of ten on offer.

"Want to share?" she asked, and in that moment, immediately became their friend.

Her first smoke, like theirs, was not an unqualified success. She coughed uncontrollably as the heat caught her throat, paled as the nicotine surged through her bloodstream like an alien invader. Deirdre persisted, though, and for six months she joined them every day. Her paper round funded her habit, and, to an extent, theirs; she gave away more sticks than she ever received.

When she didn't turn up any more, it was a week before they thought to enquire. Charles had hardly noticed. He had a new girlfriend, his first in fact, and was spending less time with his friends. Richard and Tim missed Deirdre's cigarettes. "What's up with your sister?" Richard asked young Davey when they encountered him outside the science block.

Davey shrugged, and said he supposed she was revising for exams. She was always complaining how difficult her studies were. Girls, and sisters in particular, were a mystery to him, and a matter of indifference.

Charles forgot all about her as his life swept him away from his childhood in Chislehurst, to a job in the City, marriage and a family. Decades later, to his chagrin, he found himself living with his parents again. Of his old friends, only Tim still lived locally. He'd never married. They met for an occasional drink after work, a welcome respite from stilted conversation with his parents, culminating in Tim's suggestion they try clubbing together.

There was nothing wrong with the nightclub in Bromley that Tim chose, it just wasn't Charles' scene. He preferred a pub serving craft beer, ideally without a side order of pounding disco music. Tim was obviously a regular, for he spotted a group of women as they entered and nudged Charles in the ribs. "Strangers in town."

"Fresh meat, are they?" Charles said drily.

"Oh, yes," Tim leered.

There were four of them, all blonde, long limbed and well into their thirties. That was only to be expected. Tim, a teacher, had deliberately chosen a club with a more mature clientele. There was nothing worse, he said, than bumping into your sixth formers on the dancefloor.

"Let them get tanked up, then move in there," Tim said.

The women were seated around a table, sharing two pitchers of a lurid blue drink. Charles and Tim bought their beer, a branded lager that Charles would normally avoid, and found seats nearby.

"How's the single life suiting you, Charles?" Tim asked.

"Fine." Charles lied. He'd rather have been settling down on the sofa in front of the TV with Rachel. He still didn't understand why she'd decided she no longer wanted to be married.

"They're looking our way," Tim said.

The most gorgeous of the four, a woman in a tight red dress, was staring in their direction. She spoke briefly to her friends. They laughed, joining her in looking at the men. She waved.

"Come hither," Tim said, with a satisfied smirk. He rose to his feet. "Up you get, Charlie. Let's have a chat with the lady in red."

She flashed a dazzling smile as they approached. "It's Chas, isn't it? And that can't be Timbo, surely?"

Nobody had used their childhood nicknames since they left school. "The very same," Tim replied. "Forgive me. You are?"

"Don't you remember? Dee from the Smokers' Corner."

Charles searched his memory banks. "Davey Saxton's big sister." Vague recollections began to coalesce.

"That's right." Deirdre flashed a perfect set of pearly white teeth. "And here's Jackie, Lisa and Liz. We won the hockey trophy the year you left."

"Dee was our captain," Lisa said.

Charles was astounded. Prompted, he just about recognised the others, but not Deirdre. She must be in her early forties, but she looked ten years younger. Her puppy fat, acne and mousy hair were gone. She'd become slender and peachy-skinned, her hair sleek and blonde.

"What brings you out for a night in Bromley, Chas?" Deirdre asked.

"Er, just a night out." Charles was aware it was a feeble answer, but he was unnerved by Tim's irritated expression. Perhaps his friend had earmarked Deirdre for himself. That was too bad. Tim would have to settle for Jackie, Lisa or Liz, or even all three if they were so inclined. "Would you like to dance?" he asked.

The strident music was hardly conducive to a slow dance, but she agreed. "Wouldn't you prefer a cigarette?" she suggested, as they headed for the dancefloor.

They asked at the bar, and were directed to the rather unpleasant concrete garden reserved for smokers.

"I don't smoke, actually," she said, as he lit up.

"When did you give up?" he asked, wondering why she'd chosen to go outside in that case. Perhaps she simply needed fresh air. He noted she still boasted an ample chest, but took care to make eye contact. He'd developed some self-restraint since his adolescence.

30

"Oh, not long after I began," Deirdre said. "You started to go out with Becky Ogden, so there wasn't a lot of point."

"Sorry?" He couldn't make the connection.

"I only smoked to get close to you," she said. "I wanted to be your friend."

"You were," he reassured her. "You were just like one of the chaps. Timbo, Dicky, you and me." He saw her crestfallen expression, and realised at last what she was saying. "I'm sorry," he said, "I was dense then and evidently I'm not much better now. I didn't twig at all." Even if he had, it wouldn't have made any difference then. She just hadn't been his type, certainly not by comparison with reed-slim Becky. Now, though, was another matter altogether.

"You haven't changed a bit. I can't believe it. It's lovely to see you after all these years," Deirdre gushed.

"Ditto," Charles said. He knew he was in good shape, only a few wrinkles around his blue eyes betraying his age, but it was gratifying to hear it all the same. "I suppose you still live around here?"

Deirdre laughed. "No, in London. I rarely come back, but Jackie wanted to celebrate her birthday in a nightclub. Like the old days."

"Why not a hedonistic night in London?"

"Well, we wanted to pay tribute to our teens," Deirdre said. "Dolling ourselves up for a nightspot in Bromley, drinking cocktails, dancing round our handbags – we couldn't have been classier twenty five years ago."

"You certainly look classy now," he said appreciatively.

"Thank you," Deirdre said. "You've nearly finished your cigarette, and I still know so little about you. I thought you were going to be a professional footballer. Did it happen?"

"We all had dreams, I guess." He sighed. "No, I went into banking."

"Davey didn't make it either. He works for an insurance company. Lives in the suburbs with a wife and four children."

31

"I settled down with a wife and a semi in Brockenhurst. Our daughter's in her last year of university. But my wife and I are no longer together."

"I'm sorry to hear that." She actually looked sympathetic. "Is there a girlfriend on the scene?"

"No. That wasn't why we split." He totally understood why she wanted to know. "I've moved back with my parents." He stubbed out the cigarette. "Shall we return to the dancefloor?"

"Not yet," Deirdre said. "First, I'm going to do what I should have done when I was fourteen." She flung her arms around his neck and kissed him.

Charles was shocked for a second or two. Having decided in that brief moment that he liked it, he reciprocated avidly. His tongue, flicking towards her lips, found her mouth entirely willing. He clasped her body towards him, feeling her yield.

Deirdre pulled away from him, her eyes sparkling like diamonds. "Let's get a taxi back to my place," she suggested.

Charles' mouth was agape. He'd rather hoped for this outcome, but he'd expected it to happen somewhat later. "You don't waste any time, do you?" he said. "It won't look good if we leave this early, in front of all our friends."

"The girls said I should go for it," Deirdre pointed out.

That just left Tim. Charles had the dubious pleasure of saying, "I've pulled, mate. You're on your own." Luckily, Tim didn't appear too upset. He was enjoying the company of the erstwhile hockey stars.

Deirdre ordered a cab through Uber. "I live alone," she told him.

"Have you been married?" he asked.

"I never found the right guy."

They chatted and cuddled throughout the journey. She told him she wasn't academic like her brother, she was a fitness and yoga instructor, and much of her business was done online. Charles was so absorbed in her physical presence, her words barely registered. He paid little attention to the cab's route either, imagining Deirdre would live in one of the nearer environs of London; Penge or Dulwich perhaps. To his surprise, they were whisked across Westminster Bridge, ending their journey in a stuccoed square shortly afterwards.

The huge white houses, like giant wedding cakes, looked quietly opulent. Deirdre's flat was a lateral apartment, occupying the first floor of two adjacent villas. Dramatic in shades of grey and white, it was scented by bouquets of lilies.

"Not bad for a yoga teacher," Charles said, overawed. "Is there anything I should know?"

He'd made the assumption that a rich man would have paid for the sumptuous flat, although there was no evidence of male occupation. The brocades, velvets and carved furniture were decidedly feminine. In any event, Deirdre chose to ignore his question.

"Would you like a drink?" she asked.

He took her in his arms. "I'm more interested in other things."

"Me too," Deirdre admitted. "I want to make up for lost time."

He'd moved in the next day. Her sole condition had been to insist he smoked only on the balcony.

Fifteen months later, he was still with her, still heading for the balcony when he needed nicotine. His cigarette was reaching its end now. Mark's, he saw, was already finished. "Definitely no silver spoons," Charles said. "Dee and Davey Saxton were brought up in a semi in Chislehurst, same as me."

"Haven't they done well for themselves?" Mark said.

The unspoken assumption, Charles supposed, was that he had not. He felt he had done his duty in talking to Mark. "I'm meeting my daughter for dinner at eight," he said, placing the cigarette stub in an ashtray discreetly fixed to the railings. "Let me introduce you to more of Dee's guests." On her laptop, Deirdre would have a list of invitees, colour-coded by common interests. She was ferociously well-organised. If he could somehow access that list, perhaps under the guise of checking sporting fixtures, he could divert Mark towards suitable individuals.

Deirdre saved him the bother. "Hey," she said, as he re-entered her splendid rococo drawing room, "I've been looking for you two. Mark, you need to meet Camilla over there." She pointed to a strikingly beautiful, and very bored-looking, young brunette.

"I really should be going, Dee," Charles said, suspecting he would have a mere few seconds to talk to her alone.

"You could manage another ten minutes," she said.

"The traffic will be bad."

His anxiety must have been evident, because she changed her mind. "Of course, you're seeing Amy." She hugged him and kissed each cheek, just as she had for each guest as they arrived and would undoubtedly do again when they departed. Gesturing around the busy room, she said, "This will be finished in an hour. Leave room for a glass of wine with me later."

The caterers would tidy the flat, he knew. Deirdre had used them before. Her little black book of contacts was second to none. When he returned, the drawing room would be pristine and tranquil, and they would snuggle up on the sofa with a bottle of fizz to celebrate.

His car was garaged in a mews round the corner. Charles smoked another cigarette on his way, his excitement mounting. The Porsche was new. Deirdre had seen him staring at it as they walked past the dealership and had urged him to buy it. He only complied because he was afraid she would make a gift of it to him, and he couldn't bear that. Despite his affection for her, Charles already felt like a rich woman's lapdog. The car was everything he desired, though: shiny, sleek and smooth. He still felt a pleasurable thrill at the thought of driving it. Opening the garage door, he stroked the car's gleaming white paintwork.

Driving it was even better than admiring it, although the early evening traffic cramped his style. The Porsche could do 0-60 in four seconds. While there was little opportunity to try in London, the car came into its own at Hyde Park Corner. Ignoring the grim faces of cab drivers as he cut across them, he accelerated onto the roundabout in the most satisfying way. He could feel their envy, and revelled in it.

Amy was waiting outside the main door of her office, staring down at her feet and scowling. It was a busy road with double yellow lines and he shouldn't really stop there. Glancing around quickly for police and seeing none, he flicked on the hazard lights and halted smoothly in front of her.

He was about to run his fingers through his hair, a nervous reaction, then remembered it was spiked and gelled. "Hop in."

"Take a lift from you? In your new sports car? I don't want anyone thinking I'm your girlfriend."

Charles hoped she was speaking in jest. Just in case, he played it with a straight bat. "Don't be silly. It's obvious I'm your father." This was not quite true, he realised. Amy's ginger hair was a throwback to previous generations, a shock both to him and Rachel when their daughter was born. His own locks were dark, apart from a few grey strands which he removed whenever he spotted them. His personality, too, was different. He was inclined to compromise, eager to please; a characteristic that had led to his ill-advised early marriage.

"No, that's a mid-life crisis car. I'm embarrassed to be seen in it." Amy obviously wasn't joking. Was she deliberately being hurtful? He'd thought the barbed remarks and spikiness had vanished with her adolescence. Evidently, they were simply simmering below the surface before staging a reappearance.

Charles admitted defeat. "All right," he said. "I'll park round the corner."

He regretted it as they walked together to New Change, the sybaritic air conditioning of the car replaced by stifling London air heavy with exhaust fumes. Although they were outside for a few minutes only, Charles was perspiring freely when they arrived at Amy's chosen destination.

He'd suggested a wine bar by the Thames, one of Deirdre's favourites. Amy had other ideas. She wanted to be taken to a barbecue restaurant. It was a modish place where the other customers were at least a decade younger than Charles. The menu featured a short and deceptively cheap list of main dishes, to which could be added many extras at an extortionate price. Nevertheless, he encouraged Amy to pile her plate. He had done this since she first left home for university, convinced she wouldn't eat otherwise. While she was now working in the City and hadn't followed him into nicotine addiction, a vice common among his slimmer female colleagues, she seemed unnaturally thin and pale.

"How's your new flatmate?" he asked.

"Kat's not really new any more, Dad," Amy said. "We've been sharing for two months."

"What's she like?" he persisted.

"Tidy," Amy said. "I suppose that's what you really want to know?" Her eyes were dreamy. "Kat's fun. She likes to hear about my world, although hers is much more exciting. She's a croupier in a top casino and she meets celebs all the time. We go to amazing parties thanks to the invitations that come her way. She's got a tall, dark and handsome boyfriend too."

"Is he a 'celeb' – the boyfriend?" Charles asked.

"Who, Jeb? No, Kat calls him an East End gangster. I suppose he's not really her boyfriend, more a wannabe. He never stays over. But he takes her out on the town a lot."

Charles was rather alarmed. "I think I should visit your flat and meet her."

Amy resisted a parental inspection. "No Dad, there's no room for visitors. That's why we go out so much. My bedroom has no space for a wardrobe, let alone a chair you could sit on. I have to hang my clothes on hooks on the wall."

"Isn't there a living room or a kitchen?"

"Neither. We have what's called a kitchenette, and it's a cupboard. Kat sleeps in the lounge. I mean, it's a one bedroom flat. She shouldn't really be subletting to me, but it's what everyone does to make ends meet."

"You're paying nearly a thousand pounds a month for that?" He was horrified.

"What else can I do? Fitzrovia is a nice area, and it's close enough to work. Parveen expects me at her beck and call 24-7. I couldn't carry on living in Hendon. It was cheaper, but it took too long to get back from work. And it wasn't safe late at night, when Parveen finally released me from my toil."

Charles shuddered. "Did anything..."

"No." She interrupted him firmly. "And you're not to say a word to Mum. She's already guilt-tripping me about living away from home. She thinks I should spend all my salary commuting from Brockenhurst instead of paying rent to live in London."

"There's no chance I'll tell her anything," Charles said ruefully. "Rachel won't speak to me. She threw me out, remember?"

"She would have taken you back if you hadn't shacked up with your long-term lover."

"I doubt it," Charles said. "She made it clear our marriage was over." He stared at her, seeing Rachel in the graceful oval shape of her face, then his own long-lashed eyes mirrored in hers. Since she'd been born, he'd been besotted with her, fascinated by this person who was a blend of her parents and yet very much herself. He added, "And Deirdre's not my long-term lover. I hadn't seen her since I left school. It was pure chance that we met after the split." He shivered at the word, his memory still raw.

Amy appeared to soften. "I know none of this is your fault," she said.

"There's no chance of going back, I'm afraid," Charles said gently.

"I wish you'd kept your old car, though," she said. "I was going to ask if you could help me with the deposit for a flat."

"I took out a huge loan to buy the car. Anyway, what kind of flat could you afford?" On her salary, even a studio in Fitzrovia was a stretch. Property was so pricy now. At Amy's age, he'd been able to buy a semi in Brockenhurst. He'd needed it, with Rachel suddenly pregnant and a registry office wedding hastily arranged. Young people wanted everything on a plate these days, of course. Take Alex, his boss who'd recently had a lavish stag weekend in Berlin with lederhosen and lager all round. Charles had counted himself lucky to have a pub crawl in Chislehurst, at the end of which he'd legged it home to avoid being handcuffed to a lamppost.

"Perhaps when you sell the house, our house," she emphasised the last two words, "then you can help me buy somewhere."

"Your mother rather expects me to pay for a cottage for her."

"But you'll have money left over?"

"For myself. I'd like a place of my own."

"Dad," she wheedled, "you don't need one. You're living in luxury with Deirdre."

"I may not always want to live out of a suitcase at her flat." He didn't want to be dependent on a woman, or his divorce would have been pointless.

"Deirdre's loaded. Do you think she'd lend me money for a deposit, if I asked her nicely?"

"Deirdre has helped you enough. She got you into a job that most marketing graduates would kill for."

"I can't stand it."

"Welcome to my world." She was spoiled, of course; his precious only child. He laid the blame at Rachel's door. What kind of role model was she for a child: flitting in and out of part-time jobs, and now her marriage too, whining about self-fulfilment? Commuter trains at the crack of dawn, labouring long hours to please unreasonable bosses, being inconvenienced by your work – these were the necessary evils that had paid for a roof over his family's heads in an idyllic village. His daughter seemed to want a central London flat and a fabulous social life without lifting a finger for it. Of course, Deirdre had all that, but she'd worked hard to achieve it. Her online fitness programme hadn't grown into a multi-million pound business by itself. She'd put decades of hard graft into it.

His new relationship was serving its purpose. Slowly, he was recovering from the devastation Rachel had wrought by ending their marriage. More and more, though, he wondered if he'd been too quick to become part of a couple again. While he adored her Mayfair flat, the parties and holidays, he wasn't ready yet to let Deirdre lock him up with golden chains.

For one thing, although smoking had brought them together, she didn't really approve of it. He'd never given up his adolescent habit, and didn't intend to now. "Just going outside for some fresh air," he told Amy. She rolled her eyes.

Chapter 5 Amy

Amy received two texts on Saturday night: one from Kat, inviting her to a party in Bloomsbury, and another from her mother, Rachel. Would Amy like to come down on the train for Sunday lunch, Rachel wanted to know. The dog was pining for her.

Amy responded coolly to Rachel's blatant attempt at emotional blackmail, with a text explaining she was out later and would use Sunday to catch up on sleep. She thought, but didn't say, that the dog probably missed Charles even more. That hadn't stopped Rachel discarding him, having decided after twenty years that marriage and domesticity were boring.

The dog, Captain, was a sweet old thing and Amy felt a pang of regret. Concerns about his future nagged at her. Rachel, her hair newly cut and dyed, was starting to wear miniskirts and dip into internet dating. She would downsize when the house was sold. It was conceivable there would be no place for Captain in her smaller, trendier new life, and what then? Two girls in a shoebox couldn't keep a dog. Nor could Charles, an uneasy lodger in another woman's flat.

Amy's worries were soon forgotten when Kat arrived home with another young woman in tow.

"We thought we'd get changed here," Kat said. "This is Jenny, by the way."

Jenny, a leggy brunette with an extremely short haircut, tutted. "Call me January," she said peevishly. "That's my professional name."

"Sorry, January." Kat was trying, and failing, to stifle a chuckle.

"Didn't your hair catch fire this week?" Amy asked.

"Oh yes, I'm newly-shorn. It was all extensions anyway," January said. "Like my new dress? I bought it for the party." She shook out a silky black number from a Vivienne Westwood carrier bag.

Amy tried not to gasp at the price tag: seven hundred pounds. "How did you know there was a party?" she asked. "Kat only just told me."

January grinned. "I always party on a Saturday night," she said. "We have to turn the invitations away. Kat, where can I go to put this dress on?"

"You either share with me, or it's the bathroom," Kat replied.

January chose the latter. "My goodness, this place is minute!" she exclaimed. "My flat in Covent Garden is much bigger."

"How can you afford it?" Amy asked.

"My friends help," January's muffled voice said from the bathroom.

"We'd better get going," Kat said. "You're ready, aren't you, Amy? Can you zip me up, please?"

"Marc Jacobs, I see," Amy said, admiring Kat's tight green frock. Where did Kat find the money for designer labels like that? Amy's own garment, from the high street's finest, felt drab, even though she'd chosen blue to match her eyes and a short hemline to show off her legs. "We're a bit late. It's after midnight."

"That's when the party starts." January had emerged looking like a film star in her new outfit. "Anyway, we already had to beg to leave work early."

Their destination was just the other side of Tottenham Court Road. Kat had booked a cab already and it was waiting in the car park as they left.

"Just so you know," Kat said, "our host tonight is Ali, who's a student from the Gulf. He was playing blackjack and baccarat earlier with his uncle. They're not allowed to gamble or drink back home, so they like to do it here. He says their house is amazing."

"It is," January said. "They showed me pictures earlier. Ali won big at baccarat, so he's in a good mood."

They were welcomed to the tall Georgian townhouse in Gordon Square by a butler with a guest list. "Look, here we are," Kat said, pointing to the list. "January plus two."

"Very good," the flunky sniffed, crossing out the name with a fountain pen. "Please ascend to the first floor, to the drawing room at the front."

41

The party was in full swing. An effete, tuxedoed young man was playing a white baby grand. Waiters handed out cocktails to the guests, a group of good-looking girls in long dresses and mostly young and handsome men. Even so, heads turned as Kat and January entered the room in their designer dresses.

"Look, that's Craig Miller, the soap star," January cried. "Listen, girls, would you like a snort before we start?"

"Not for me," Kat said. Craig Miller had caught her eye, and she headed to his side for a chat.

Amy declined as well, grabbing a drink and downing it as quickly as possible. She'd never had the money or inclination to touch drugs. In a huff, January left her in search of a bathroom, saying acidly she hoped it would be larger than Amy's.

As champagne cocktails flowed freely, Amy relaxed. Ali, an attractive long-haired youth in his twenties, greeted her briefly and made some introductions to put her at ease. Most of the guests, she learned, were medical students like Ali or artist friends of his uncle. None of them seemed remotely interested in a date, but were willing to chat. In time, Kat joined her again.

"No luck with Craig?" Amy asked.

Kat pulled a face. "I could have gone home with him if I wanted to."

"I would have," Amy said, admiring Craig's regular features and the athletic figure revealed by his taut T-shirt. He was talking to January now, his arm around her waist. "Looks like January's about to."

"No," Kat replied. "That's who she's after." She pointed to Ali, a pretty girl hanging on each arm, and his podgy, balding uncle.

"Ali? He's surely taken already."

"His uncle," Kat said, as January disengaged from Craig and made a beeline for their hosts. "He's loaded, which is the single quality January seeks in a man. She told you her friends helped her, didn't she? I bet she didn't admit how she chooses them."

Chapter 6 Shaun

A few ghostly traces of mist clung to the Tottenham Marshes. Soon, the blazing sun would vanquish all the freshness of morning. Shaun left the main road and drove into the trading estate. He guided his Merc to the last unit in the cul-de-sac, a low, brown brick oblong surrounded by a car park. A sign below the eaves proclaimed AKD TRADING in bright yellow capitals. They were illuminated at night. The initials held no meaning for Shaun; he had simply chosen a bland, commercial-sounding name.

Shaun parked outside the front door in a space labelled 'Reserved for Directors'. Smoked glass windows revealed a man and woman sitting behind a reception desk, certificates framed on the wall behind them. Shaun pressed the buzzer.

"Come in, Mr Halloran."

The door clicked open, and he entered, wiping his shoes carefully before treading on the grey striped carpet tiles. With its light wood furniture, cheese plant and muted colours, the reception area had the appearance of a nondescript commercial premises. That was the whole point.

The twenty-something woman, her obviously augmented breasts straining within a trim black trouser suit, smiled. "Your big day today," she said, her voice betraying origins not far from Shaun's birthplace in Barking.

"Indeed. We'll be busy, Kelly," Shaun said. His excitement was rising. He had spread the word about his speakeasy within both his own milieu and the more broadminded end of the traditional business community.

Kelly made the place look even more like a conventional establishment, but she couldn't man the reception desk alone. Shaun needed a heavy, a man to spot trouble as it came through the door, and deter it with his bulk.

That man was Jeb, at least for now. While he was too valuable to be spared for long, Shaun wanted him there for the first week. Jeb knew everyone in the East End, and everyone knew him. His presence sent the right message to visitors.

"All right, boss?" Jeb said.

Shaun gave him a curt nod and allowed Kelly to buzz him through a door to the left of a certificate for the Queen's Award for Exports. Shaun enjoyed the irony. His business affairs were more geared towards imports, and the only award Her Majesty might be inclined to grant him would be detention at her pleasure.

A casual visitor would have anticipated a factory or warehouse beyond that door. Nothing could have been further from the sight that greeted Shaun, and his heart swelled with pride as he surveyed it. The cavernous space was lined with red velvet drapes. Backlit shelves held bottles of spirits above a carved wood bar, which had disappeared from an East End boozer closed for refurbishment. That pub, owned by a man who had borrowed from Shaun and refused to repay him, had unaccountably burned down.

Although the bar was surrounded by leather chesterfields, as if several sets of lounge furniture had clustered together, it was the gaming tables that took centre stage. Roulette, blackjack and poker were all on offer. Like a flock of butterflies, buxom young women in filmy dresses stood by, awaiting the gamblers who would appear within the hour.

Shaun clapped his hands to gain their attention. "Good morning. We officially open at twelve, and then I hope we never close!" He scanned the young, brightly made-up faces and leered approvingly at the croupiers' skimpy dresses. There was no uniform as such; this was more hedonistic than Diamonds and the stuffy casinos of the West End. He'd just told them to look appealing. "Don't forget. It's your job to keep the punters gambling, drinking and smoking. When they stop, get them to gamble, drink and smoke some more! Who cares what they do, as long as they're spending money. If they want to shag you, be my

44

guest. There's a room out the back for that. Just stick to the house rules when you do it: it's half for me, half for you. Cash goes to Vince at the bar. At the slightest hint that you're ripping me off, Jeb will search you. Understood?" That was threat enough for anyone; Jeb wasn't renowned for being gentle. Shaun paused as the girls nodded. "Good. Have fun."

He relaxed on one of the chesterfields. "Vince, get me an Old Fashioned."

The mixologist, a young, ginger-haired man sporting a leather waistcoat and extravagant sideburns, used tiny tongs to pick up a sugar lump. Placing it in a whisky glass, he sloshed in Angostura bitters with a flourish. Nothing in his delicate manner indicated he'd recently been released from a stretch for GBH.

Kat glided towards Shaun from one of the blackjack tables. "I take it the staff may smoke?" she said, a glint in her eye.

"Of course, on your breaks," Shaun said. He motioned to her to sit next to him. "Join me for one."

Kat removed a packet of Sobranie Cocktails from her pocket. She held out a long, thin lilac stick for him to light.

Shaun obliged, suddenly aware as he bent towards her that this was the closest he'd ever been to her. Smelling her scent and feeling her presence, sparky and alive, he was seized by the urge to take her to the back room. He lit a cigarette for himself and smoked it silently until the feeling passed.

Kat was wearing a long red dress which covered her completely while revealing her shape. She drew daintily on the cigarette as she said, "I didn't think you needed to say everything you did. These girls aren't Jeb's professionals."

"Oh?" Shaun tried not to show his surprise.

"He wouldn't release them from their normal duties. That's far more lucrative than working here. These ladies are his credit card team, the women who go shopping with stolen cards. They're good at maths. That's why he chose them."

No doubt with some prompting from her, Shaun thought. Jeb would never be that smart. "You seem to know a lot about Jeb's business," he said.

Kat flashed a smile. "He can be indiscreet when he's drunk. Or high."

"And in the bedroom?" he ventured.

"I wouldn't know."

He'd been right, then. "These girls," he said cautiously, "can they deal?"

"Can they do the job? Yes. I went to college for my training, but the basics don't take long to learn. I'll be on hand to help them until four, then I have to go back home and get changed for Diamonds." She drew on the lilac stick. "I don't suppose I'll see you there again."

"You might," he said. "But not Jeb."

Kat laughed lightly.

"How do you like my little speakeasy, by the way?" Shaun said, gesturing around the room.

"You really want to know?" Her green eyes looked into his.

Shaun felt an involuntary shiver sweep through him and hoped Kat hadn't noticed. "Yes. How does it compare to Diamonds?"

"You're aiming for a different clientele," Kat said tactfully. She blew out a smoke ring, a technique Shaun had never been able to master. "I think you have everything you need except a woman's touch."

He was tempted to say she could read his mind. "What do you mean?" he asked instead.

"The ambience is laddish. Dark leather, strip lights, sports on TV, a single tiny mirror in the ladies."

"I see," Shaun said, adding, "My wife would have spotted all that if she was still alive. She died of breast cancer three years ago." Of course, with Meg in his life, he wouldn't have needed this project. His time would have been filled with family parties, picnics in the forest, football coaching for the boys. He might even be retired now, on a

46

private beach in Marbella, watching Meg's ample bosom burst out of a bikini.

"I'm sorry," Kat said. She must have seen his eyes mist.

"It's in the past," he said, although really he was grieving for the future that had been taken away. "Anyhow, thanks for the advice." He had no intention of following it. In his world, men controlled the purse strings; they were the stars around which women orbited.

"You're welcome," she said, stubbing out the cigarette. "See you around."

"Just one thing," Shaun said. "I'd like you back next week, in case we have any issues. Can you do that?"

"You mean I may need to train replacements?" Kat asked. "Sure. You're wise to ask. The girls mostly have habits, and I don't mean like these." She pointed to the Sobranies. "You'll need to watch the cash round here like a hawk."

"Oh, I shall," Shaun said grimly.

"By the way," Kat said, "I guess you couldn't get Snow Mountain."

His eyes narrowed, flicking up to the pink-lit shelf where six other vodkas were on display. He had quite forgotten his laughing promise to stock the brand. Without considering why she should care, he resolved to keep his word. "I'll see to it," he said.

"High five," Kat said, holding up her hand.

He slapped it, staring at his own hand afterwards and then at her retreating figure. Until he'd finished another cigarette, he wished he was twenty years younger.

Chapter 7 Jeb

Jeb had just taken the condom out of its packet when the door buzzer sounded. He always used condoms, and the girls saw him as a knight in shining armour for that reason. In reality, he was protecting himself more than them. He literally didn't know where they'd been. Besides, he didn't want anyone calling him Dad, ever. His childhood had taught him dads were evil, violent drunkards.

"Aren't you going to get that?" Charlene asked.

"No way," Jeb said, looking hungrily at her firm fifteen year old body. He'd waited long enough, letting Charlene have her hit before exacting his price. Usually, he wanted payment in advance, but she hadn't brought enough cash. "I'm going to take it slow," he promised her.

The buzzer fell silent. Jeb began taking his pleasure. Charlene was tighter than most and she whimpered a lot, whether from pain or desire he didn't care. He wasn't doing this for her.

Charlene heard the knocking first. "There's someone at the door."

The thumping noise continued for ten minutes, growing louder. He heard the hinges rattle, and a man shout angrily, "Open up."

Jeb made a fist and rolled off the girl. He dragged a grubby blue dressing gown around his heavy frame. "I'll sort it," he told her, picking up a flick-knife to make sure.

He peered through the glass spyhole in the front door. It was a young Asian man, seemingly unarmed. Jeb relaxed, expecting a potential customer. "All right, don't wake the neighbours," he said, unlocking the door. It was a top floor flat in a quiet East London backwater by Epping Forest. At 11am, the neighbours were probably out at work. All the same, Jeb didn't like to draw too much attention to himself.

The man who dashed into his lounge was furious. "I want my money back," he shouted, black eyes flashing.

"Ahmed," Jeb said, recognising a previous client for one of his more specialist services. "What's wrong? Bride not to your liking? I don't offer a money back guarantee, you know." He kept the small flick-knife hidden in his fist, just in case.

"No, no," Ahmed said impatiently. "It's the police. They raided the Imperial Turban on my night off – luckily. I'd have been arrested if I'd been there, and off to prison at Yarl's Wood. They jail you and ask questions later. Everyone knows that. They were telling my boss it was a scam, a sham marriage."

"Well, of course it was a sham," Jeb said. "You don't get undying love for a – for ten grand. That's not what you tell the filth, though. What did Mo say to them?"

Ahmed didn't notice the slip. "He said me and my wife, we're very much in love. We marry and she moves in. Then she suddenly deserts me. I wait for her to come back."

"Right," Jeb said. "Word perfect." It was almost a true description of the marriage. Where it veered from reality was that, in fact, Kat had abandoned Ahmed within ten minutes of the ceremony, leaving no one under the illusion she might return.

"I want my money back," Ahmed repeated. "I paid you for a wedding, so I could stay in this country. If I can't stay, I'm taking that money with me."

"Calm down," Jeb said. "The police can't prove anything. Anyway, how do I know they've been raiding Mo's? You could be lying to scare me into giving you ten grand." He sucked his teeth. "Do you know what I do to liars?"

"They've arrested the reverend," Ahmed said.

That put a different complexion on the matter. First of all, it proved the veracity of Ahmed's story. He couldn't be telling a falsehood because the priest's fate was so easy to check. Secondly, it put Jeb at risk. True, the reverend had barely seen Jeb and was also bound to deny any wrongdoing. A mere pawn, he had been delighted at the increase in his flock as unlikely couples turned to him for instruction in

49

the ways of God. It didn't seem to occur to him that the newly-weds never set eyes on each other or his church again after marrying.

Jeb clapped a palm to his forehead. No, the vicar wasn't a problem. The danger for Jeb lay in the church's wedding register. All the names and addresses of brides and grooms were neatly summarised there. A few enquiries from Plod, and the trail would lead to him. Someone would give him away, he was sure of it.

He could play rough with Ahmed, but then the man would go straight back to the filth. Also, Ahmed and Mo had friends.

Jeb shivered. "Come back tonight. I'll have your money ready."

"I want it now."

He didn't have enough in the flat, but he knew where to find it. "I've got to go to the bank first," he lied.

"Meet me in an hour, then," Ahmed said. "Outside the Golden Turban, Mo's other place. I'm not going near the Imperial again."

Jeb nodded, recognising from the venue that Ahmed didn't trust him. The restaurant bristled with CCTV cameras. There was no chance of pulling a knife on Ahmed there, even if Jeb had wanted to. "You'll get your money," he said.

As soon as Ahmed left, he returned to the bedroom. Charlene still lay naked on his bed. "Give me a quick blow job," he commanded. "I'm in a hurry."

Once she'd obliged, he was in a better mood. "Want a lift?" he asked. "I'm going your way."

His beamer was parked in a lock-up round the corner. Jeb placed a friendly arm around Charlene's shoulder as he led her to it. "You know," he said to her, once they were sitting in the car and there was no danger of being overheard, "you give good head. You could be making money out of that. Just think about it. I'll always help you."

She looked up at him, her eyes unfocused. "Yeah, I'll think about it," she said.

She'd come running to his door when she needed a hit, Jeb thought, pleased to have sowed the seeds for another little money-spinner. He dropped Charlene just off the High Road on his way to Tottenham, congratulating himself. If he wanted to make it big, have an empire like Shaun's, he had to take every opportunity he could. One day, he'd have a mansion in Wanstead like his boss. Not those good-for-nothing sons, though.

It was nearly twelve when he arrived at AKD Trading. The speakeasy had been open for a week. Jeb had sat at the reception desk, twiddling his thumbs for five days until Shaun told him there was no longer any need. He'd found someone else to do door security. As Shaun's right hand man, Jeb could be expected to visit the premises to check nothing was amiss, though. Armed with that cover story, he would speak quietly to Kat and access the cash Vince always left locked in a back room.

Jeb breathed a sigh of relief when he was admitted beyond the reception desk. While a few early punters were clustered around one of the roulette tables, Shaun wasn't there. He knew Shaun was supposed to be seeing his white van man that afternoon, but you never knew for sure. Shaun was capable of changing his mind. AKD was his passion; he was like a child with a new toy.

"All good in the hood, Vince?" Jeb asked the ginger-haired barman.

"Sure," Vince said. "The place was packed out last night. I took six grand behind the bar alone."

"Is Kat around?"

"Should be here any minute," Vince said.

"Tell her I need to see her in the office," Jeb said. "You got the keys?"

Vince handed them over.

There was no safe, just a desk with a drawer that Jeb swiftly unlocked. To his dismay, the drawer appeared to be filled with A4 notepads. Jeb cursed, then saw the edge of a banknote peeping out below the stationery. Bundles of notes were neatly stacked underneath. He took most of the fifty pound notes, laboriously counting them. Tearing several pages from a notepad, he crumpled them and stuck them under the rest of the pads to provide an illusion of bulk. His haul was just over twenty thousand pounds; more than enough for Ahmed, with plenty left for a few nights on the town. He'd just finished stuffing the banknotes in his pockets and underpants when Kat knocked on the door.

"Come in." Jeb deliberately looked downcast.

"What's wrong?" Kat asked.

"The Rev. He's told the law. I'm getting out of town," Jeb said, "and I suggest you do the same. Here's a grand. Take that and go back up north. That's where you come from, isn't it?" He reached into his jacket pocket. He had counted out exactly twenty of the fifty pound notes for her.

Kat looked shocked. Her usual equilibrium deserted her. Silently, she took the cash from him.

"Cheer up; it may never happen," Jeb said. "Not as long as you lie low."

"I don't want any trouble from the police," Kat said.

"Who does?" Jeb said. He wasn't sure if he was more afraid of the police or Shaun. If you annoyed the filth, they sent you to gaol rather than tying bricks to your ankles and inviting you to take a late night swim in the river. He was confident Shaun would never know he'd stolen the money, though. Even if the theft were noticed, Kat was an obvious scapegoat. There was every chance of slipping the cash back secretly if he had a good win on the horses, anyway. Jeb smiled reassuringly at Kat. "Just finish your work here, then get out of town. I'll send the girls into the office to see you."

"Okay."

He left her in a subdued state. "Lock up after Kat, will you?" he commanded Vince. Vince stared at him for a second, then shrugged his shoulders. It was rare for anyone who knew Jeb to start an argument with him.

In the safety of his beamer, behind smoked glass windows, Jeb placed exactly ten thousand pounds in a carrier bag, locking the rest in the glove box. He'd never double-crossed Shaun before, apart from keeping the wedding scam a secret so he didn't have to give Shaun a cut. Fear suddenly gripped his throat, and he knew even the Marlboro Man wouldn't be enough to steady his nerves. Before he set off for the Golden Turban, he snorted a pinch of white powder.

Chapter 8 Shaun

Shaun's white van team had just returned from Belgium. "What've you got?" he asked Jerry, the driver.

"Lots of that strong Belgian lager you asked for," Jerry said. "Bought it cheap – special offers."

Shaun nodded. They'd run out of lager at AKD by Sunday morning; he'd had to send Vince to the cash and carry to fetch more. "Spirits?" he asked. "I wanted more premium brands this time. Snow Mountain vodka, malt whisky."

Jerry scowled. "No Snow Mountain vodka. The warehouses don't sell it. I bought Smirnoff as usual."

Shaun sighed. "All right. Let's take a look at your haul."

Scott, Jerry's mate, was unloading from the van into the storage unit they used about half a mile from AKD. He grinned. "It's all here, boss. Vodka, rum, whisky, gin."

They were the mass market brands that always sold well in the car parks of pubs and clubs. Not quite what Shaun had in mind for AKD, but he could always send the Transit boys on more frequent trips across the Channel. Jerry and Scott would do anything if the money was right, and it was a pleasant lifestyle for them; a couple of nights boozing in Bruges before they picked up the bootlegged liquor. They both had paunches to prove it. Shaun recalled the days he'd played truant with them. As teenagers, Jerry and Scott had been thin as rakes; now they were all showing their age.

He filled his car boot with crates of beer and boxes of spirits for the speakeasy. "Have a rest today and start flogging the stuff around Walthamstow tomorrow," he told them.

It was three o'clock, just time to catch Kat before she left AKD. He had no need of her services there again, which was a pity. On a whim, he stopped at an off licence and asked for Snow Mountain. They didn't have it – distribution was restricted to high end outlets, they said unashamedly – but they gave him the importer's name: Bridges.

He called them. The phone was answered with the single word, "Bridges."

"Can I speak to the boss?"

"It's Marty Bridges speaking." He was somewhere up north; his vowels flatter and consonants more pronounced than in Shaun's everyday world.

"I want to order Snow Mountain vodka for my club," Shaun said.

"Sorry, I've got a full order book."

Shaun was dumbfounded. Just for once, he was offering to buy alcohol legitimately, and the seller wasn't interested. "You don't know who you're talking to," he said. "I've a mind to come round to see you."

Bridges' tone remained offhand. "You're welcome to visit, but you won't change my mind," he said. "I can't buy enough of that product to satisfy demand. I supply it to longstanding customers only." He gave Shaun an address in Birmingham, repeating that he was happy to meet and asking if Shaun might like a different vodka.

Shaun admitted defeat. He had little interest in anywhere beyond the M25. Like Jeb, all he knew of Birmingham was that it was north of London and south of Scotland. He couldn't be bothered to travel there, or indeed send Jeb, to rough up the arrogant businessman. Returning to AKD, he looked eagerly for Kat among the gaming tables.

"Where is she?" he asked Vince.

"Kat? She left early," Vince said.

"Shame," Shaun said. He would have to return to Diamonds to see her, he supposed.

Chapter 9 Marty

Marty Bridges put down the phone. He had little time for Cockneys, especially shady nightclub owners. While he had no evidence that his caller was anything other than a hard-working businessman, he had a sixth sense that usually served him well. Erik, for instance, was straight as an arrow.

He saw Erik every month, allegedly to collect the modest rent he charged the young man, but also because he wanted to be sure Erik was keeping body and soul together. He owed it to Sasha. Although Erik's sister would always land on her feet, Erik was a dreamer and idealist like his father.

Marty had been toying with the thought of walking to the old workshop where Erik lived. It was less than two miles away and he still retained a basic level of fitness from his decades as an amateur boxer. Instead, with the sun grilling his bald head as soon as he stepped outside the office, he decided to drive. It would be cooler – he could have a quiet pint afterwards and head home when the rush hour was easing.

He counted himself lucky to find a pay and display space. Parking was heavily restricted in Birmingham's Jewellery Quarter nowadays. He remembered when it was called Hockley. It was rough as a hedgehog's bottom then; he had picked up the workshop for a song at auction.

Now his tenants, artisan jewellers, had moved out, he wanted to redevelop the site. Many of the area's handsome red-brick buildings had already been converted into homes, bars and media offices. The quirky Victorian Gothic properties appealed to yuppies. Marty was hoping for a substantial profit once he'd cleared the red tape. "I've been turned down for planning permission again," he complained to Erik.

Erik nodded, in that attentive way of his. He sipped a mug of tea. They were sitting in the lounge, a large but shabby space that had once been used to display stock. Marty sank into his armchair, noting it was still well-sprung. Erik's lodgings might be draughty and basic – there was no bath or shower, and only a tiny kitchen – but there was plenty of space, and the furniture was of good quality. Most of it had been discarded from Marty's house, and he didn't buy cheap rubbish.

He studied the younger man, noting Erik's thin face and nose, his whippet skinniness and the dark, spiky hair that was starting to recede from his high forehead. He was the image of Sasha at the same age. When he spoke, his words were exactly those Sasha would have used.

"Don't give up," Erik said. "Look for a different way. What do the planners want?" He had a very upper crust voice, the legacy of a childhood at English boarding schools. Sasha, who always spoke English with a strong accent, would have been proud of him.

"I don't know." Marty grimaced, letting his frustration show. "I just want to convert the building into flats. It's already been done for several other factories in this very street, so I can't see a problem. But both designs I've submitted have been rejected."

"What reasons did they give?" Erik's interest probably went beyond idle curiosity. After all, Marty wouldn't need a caretaker living in the property once it had been redeveloped.

"They didn't like the proposed cellar conversion. I dropped that, and applied again. The second time, they said they wanted to retain industrial use. Crazy. This road isn't an industrial zone."

"I wonder," Erik said, his face tight with concentration, "perhaps they were worried about the tunnel in the cellar."

Marty sat bolt upright, intrigued. He'd toured every nook and cranny of the old building, or so he believed. "What tunnel?" he asked.

"Didn't you know?" Erik looked surprised. "There's a door at one end of the cellar, behind some metal racking the jewellers left. It leads to another room, with a vertical shaft and ladder descending into the earth."

Marty whistled. "And? Did you climb down the ladder?"

Erik shook his head.

"I don't understand why my architects never spotted that door," Marty said.

"There was a lot of junk in the way," Erik pointed out. "Do you want to take a look now?"

"Yes, and find out what's at the bottom of the shaft," Marty agreed. He switched on his smartphone flashlight.

The cellar itself was accessed from a door in the hallway, from which stone steps led to a bare-earthed room, roughly oblong but narrowing considerably at one end. This was obscured by white-painted metal racking, grey with dust and piled with rusted tools and machinery.

Marty's eyes widened. "It's behind that?" he said. "How on earth did you get past all that rubbish, or, for that matter, find a door in the first place?"

"I wanted to build a coffee table and I was looking for parts," Erik said. "That was when I noticed the door. As for access – well, I'll show you."

He removed the rusty detritus from the bottom shelf, crouched down and wriggled through to the gap beyond, appearing to expand like a rubber band as he stood up.

Only another man as slim as Erik could hope to follow. "Okay," Marty said, drawing out the word slowly. "I'll be stuck in the racking if I try that. Want to explain to the fire brigade?"

"Why don't you give me your phone?" Erik suggested. "I could use that torch, and I'll take a few snaps for you."

Marty listened, intensely curious, as the door creaked open. He heard the dull clang of Erik's feet on the metal tread, as the last rays from the torch dimmed and disappeared.

"It's about twenty metres deep," Erik reported back, "with a locked steel door at the bottom." They returned to the living room and he poured more tea as Marty inspected the photographs.

"Odd," Marty said. "It could be a way into Anchor." He noted Erik's perplexed expression. "You don't know what I'm talking about do you? It's way before your time, and mine too, come to that. Anchor is an old complex of telecommunications tunnels under the Jewellery Quarter and city centre. It was built as an underground train network sixty years ago, then shelved before it was finished. I remember my father talking about it."

"You said telecoms," Erik pointed out.

"That's what they used it for in the end," Marty said. "At least, as far as I know. There are a lot of secrets in those tunnels. Government secrets. You and I wouldn't be allowed in there. If it's a gateway to Anchor that explains why the planners don't want it disturbed."

"Can't you tell them you'll pour concrete down the shaft?" Erik asked.

"Who knows?" Marty said. "Perhaps not. It may be required for ventilation. All I know is, as it's classified information, the planners won't tell me whether this is Anchor or not. I can try my council contacts, but I'm not holding my breath."

"Auntie Lizzie could tell you, I bet," Erik said. "Her husband was a telecoms engineer."

"There's a thought," Marty said. "Perhaps the old bag does know." He sighed. "I doubt she'd tell me."

"I could ask her," Erik said. "We're still in touch."

"Don't mention my name," Marty said. He scowled. "Do you fancy a drink at the Rose Villa Tavern?"

"Sure, why not?" Erik said. "I work behind the bar for one of their rivals, but I can sneak in wearing dark glasses."

"Bar work? Is that all you're doing these days, after studying all those years?" Marty was genuinely horrified. Despite the recession, his business had thrived, as had his children's careers.

"Yes, that's what I do to pay your extortionate rent," Erik replied, tongue in cheek. "And it also funds my passion, which is to cure cancer."

Marty stared at him, open-mouthed. There had been enough surprises today already. Surely this was a joke? Yet the tunnel hadn't been a prank. Erik had never looked more serious.

"You've heard stories about remote valleys where people live for many, many years? An unusual number of centenarians. There is one such in my homeland. More of a mountain pass than a valley. My father used to take me skiing there."

Marty couldn't avoid displaying his scepticism. "Forgive me, Erik. Surely the paperwork in these remote places is so poor they don't know how old anyone really is? As a scientist, I'm surprised you give these rumours any credit."

Erik rolled his eyes. "You think I was brought up in a mud hut? I spent months there as a child, seeing with my own eyes that some families had five or six generations still living. I've checked up on them. The birth, marriage and death certificates are all consistent. They either don't suffer from the Big C, or they get it and recover from it. The single difference between their lifestyles and ours is the tea they drink every morning. They make it from the leaves of a local shrub, darria. I've been able to isolate the active ingredient."

"I believe you," Marty said, gathering his thoughts, "but only because I know you, Erik. If it was anyone else spinning me a line about a miracle tea, I'd show them the door." His mind was rapidly running through the ramifications of Erik's discovery. "This is wonderful news, both for society and for you. You realise it has commercial possibilities? With the right marketing behind you, this darria tea could make you a millionaire."

"That's not what I want," Erik said, unexpectedly.

"Why not? The more people buy it, the more you're helping them," Marty said, puzzled and somewhat disappointed. If Erik wasn't interested in making sales, there wouldn't be much chance of a profit for anyone else.

"Maybe a few thousand enlightened people would drink darria tea. Perhaps a few hundred thousand, with the right press coverage. Not all of them will drink enough. Some will dislike the taste, others get bored with it after a week. But if I apply scientific rigour, I can turn the active ingredient into a drug that will save millions of lives."

Marty stroked his chin. He could see this approach would make more money, but the upfront costs would be higher. "I thought drugs needed clinical trials – tests so expensive, only deep-pocketed pharmaceuticals companies can afford them."

"They do," Erik admitted. "I had to call in favours to run an initial set of clinical trials. My university contacts did a lot of the work for free, and I nevertheless spent every penny I had. But it was worth it, because the darria was proved to work."

"What next?" Marty asked. "When are you going into production?"

Erik shook his head. "It's not so simple. I need to extend the clinical trials to get regulatory approval. That's where it gets costly. I could sell my patent to Big Pharma, but then they'll charge a fortune for the drug. The people who need it will be denied treatment. I must find another way."

Purely by chance, Erik could have stumbled on a goldmine. He needed a sensible business partner. "I can help you there," Marty said. "I'd invest in a joint venture with you, like the way I built the Snow Mountain vodka brand with your father. Interested?"

Erik's serious face broke into a rare smile of excitement. "Definitely."

"Well then," Marty said, "can you show me the results so far? Then we'll go out for that pint, and seal the deal."

"Of course; it's all on my laptop," Erik said. "Wait here." He motioned to Marty to sit on the sofa, a battered but comfortable red leather piece which had served Marty's children well in their playroom.

Erik disappeared into his bedroom. Marty began to consider how to fund the darria research. His trading business, initially just Snow Mountain vodka and now encompassing many other exclusive imported brands, consistently generated surplus cash. He had invested most of it in assets like this one, however: unloved buildings ripe for redevelopment. While he could use them as security for loans, he'd be able to borrow more and on better terms once planning permission was obtained. That made it even more vital to solve the mystery of the cellar.

"I left my laptop on the bus!" Erik emerged from his bedroom, ashen-faced. "It isn't here, and I know what must have happened. I helped an old woman alight from the bus at my stop, and I left my bags on the seat next to me."

That was so typical of Erik that Marty had to struggle to suppress a grin. "You've got back-ups, though?" he asked. "In the cloud, right?"

"Not in the cloud," Erik said. "I don't trust it. I used a USB stick, which was in the same bag as my laptop."

"You mean all the data's gone, and anyone could have it?" Marty, so hopeful of profiting from the darria venture, was shocked. He was glad his heart was in a healthy state.

"No and no," Erik said, to Marty's relief. "My sister keeps a spare USB stick at her flat in Fitzrovia. I mail one to her every fortnight. And I encrypt everything, so there's no danger of anyone else seeing it." He looked at his watch. "I'd still like to show it to you as soon as possible, Marty. I'm going to forego that pint and go to London now."

"Can you afford the train fare?" Marty asked, preparing to dip into his pocket.

"No, I'll travel by coach," Erik replied.

"Don't be silly," Marty said. He took a hundred pounds from his wallet and handed the cash to his new business partner. "Call it a down-payment. I'm sure I can find an old laptop for you too, back at my office."

Erik looked at him quizzically.

"I trust you," Marty said. "You can trust me too; you should know that by now. Please give my regards to your sister. Swanky Fitzrovia, eh?" He whistled. "I'm not surprised she lives there; a cat always lands on its feet. By the way, if you can find out more from Lizzie when you come back, it will help both of us."

Erik hesitated for a second, then held out his right hand. His handshake was firm. "You can count on me," he said.

Marty nodded. He was sure Erik would be more careful with his data in future. Still, the Rose Villa Tavern had seldom seemed more inviting.

Chapter 10 Amy

Dusk was falling as Amy left work. Even if she took the Central Line, it would be ten before she was home. She mentally rehearsed the speech she would make at work when she won the lottery. She was nearly word perfect now. 'Gather round everyone, and join me for a glass of champagne. I've brought in a caseful to glug. What's that you say, we're not allowed to take drink into work? It's a sackable offence? That's a shame, because I so wanted to tell Parveen she could stick her job. Where can she stick it, you ask? Up her saggy bottom. And then she can move that fat arse and do some work for a change. You can swallow a live frog, can't you, Parveen?'

It was in danger of becoming a rant. Perhaps she would omit the champagne for her colleagues. Corporate clones to a man, they hardly deserved any. She would just explain all of Parveen's faults to her. The short Tube journey passed pleasantly enough as she planned what to say.

Parveen had ordered pizzas to be brought to the office, which fortunately saved the cost of a microwaved ready meal and meant Amy could go straight to bed on arriving home. Changing into a thin T-shirt nightie, she brushed her hair and applied soap and water to the day's smudged make-up. She cleaned her teeth and drank a glass of water. Only when she lay under her duvet, enjoying the blissful coolness it offered for the first few minutes, did she hear Kat.

At least, she assumed it was Kat. Occasional footsteps and thuds could be heard through the thin partition wall. Kat would usually be at work all evening. If she weren't, it would be fun to gossip for a few minutes. Amy was curious, too, to know what was absorbing Kat so much that she hadn't heard her flatmate return. She rose from the narrow bed, tiptoed into the corridor and knocked on the door of Kat's bedroom. "Kat?" she called.

There was no reply. Suppose the noise was being made by an intruder? Amy hastily returned to her room and threw on some clothes, picking up her phone and keys in case she needed to run for help. Gingerly, she opened Kat's door a crack.

The stranger in the bedroom spun round immediately. "Who are you?" he said.

He made no move towards her, perhaps because he was holding two potted plants in his hands. She opened the door fully to take a look at him. He was young, perhaps in his late twenties, tall, thin and pale with short spiky black hair. His clothes were unremarkable: a black bomber jacket and jeans. She might have passed him at a Tube station without a second glance. That nondescript appearance, of course, would serve a burglar well, but his words and voice were not those of a burglar. He spoke like many of Amy's colleagues, particularly Ross; a tone redolent with privilege, penthouse flats and a public school education.

"I'm Amy," she said, suddenly self-conscious. Her comprehensive schooling had produced a different sound, of a sort that he and his friends might consider second-rate. That was how Ross perceived it, she was sure. "I'm Kat's flatmate. Who are you and what are you doing here?"

He ignored her questions. "Where's Kat?" he asked impatiently, his green eyes staring intently into hers.

"I don't know." Kat was almost certainly at work, but Amy resolved to tell him nothing.

"I'll wait until she returns, then."

"You will not." Amy was outraged. "You have no right to be here in my flat, whoever you are."

"I have every right. Look." He put the plants down and fished in his pocket for a set of keys.

She recognised them as the front door keys for the flat. "Where did you get those?"

"From Kat, of course. I have every right to them. I've been storing my property here."

"Like those plants?" They had been sitting on Kat's windowsill, two rather unexceptional small shrubs.

He nodded, bringing the pots closer to his chest. "Yes, my magic trees. She has looked after them well, but they need more sunshine."

If she needed proof he was a little odd, here it was. Amy scrutinised the plants. They were hardly trees, really no more than a mass of twigs covered in small glossy leaves. She'd never paid much attention to them before. They weren't cannabis; she was sure of that. She'd simply assumed they'd burst into flower one day, like the showy white orchid on Kat's bookshelf.

He might have sensed her scepticism. "I'm looking for more besides. I can't find everything. She must have it."

"You'll have to come back when she's here," Amy said.

"Yes, yes." He waved a hand dismissively. "I will leave. Don't panic."

One of the young man's jeans pockets suddenly resounded with Prokofiev's Dance of the Knights, a piece Amy recognised as one of her mother's favourites. He grabbed the phone from his pocket. "Da?"

He was clearly delighted to hear from the caller. His face broke into a smile. Suddenly, instead of looking average, he was handsome. He nodded enthusiastically and spoke a few words in a foreign language.

The call over, he turned his attention back to Amy. "Okay, I'm leaving now. With these." He gestured to the pots.

She bit her lip, unsure whether to stop him, then shrugged her shoulders. What could she do? He was taller and stronger. Kat's little shrubs were really dull, anyway. The florist nearby, a cool green haven on a hot street corner, had much prettier ones. "All right," she said, praying Kat would understand.

Chapter 11 Shaun

"I want you here at once, Jeb," Shaun fumed.

"I can't drive. I've been drinking." Jeb's voice sounded muffled. He was probably still in the White Horse.

"Get a taxi." Shaun jabbed at his phone to end the call. He wanted some explanations from Jeb. Takings were suddenly down dramatically, going by the amount of cash stashed away in the office at AKD. If Vince was to be believed, however, there should be at least thirty grand there. He was twenty grand light. Vince also alleged Jeb had borrowed the office keys earlier.

Shaun puffed away furiously on a cigar, a big fat Cuban number. It might come down to Vince's word against Jeb's. Then who should he trust? In his heart, he knew the answer. There was no honour among thieves; merely loose and shifting alliances. He couldn't afford to do nothing, to be perceived as weak. They would both have to go. Vince was easy to replace; Jeb, his trusted wingman of many years, less so, but it would be possible. There were always younger, hungrier men snapping at their heels.

Jeb, when he arrived, clearly the worse for drink, put a different spin on it. "Oh Kat, what have you done?" he asked rhetorically.

Shaun looked at him warily. "What do you mean?"

"I left her in that office, didn't I?" Jeb said. He held up his hands. "I'm sorry, boss. I made a big mistake."

"She was alone in the office, with the keys?"

"No, not with the keys." Jeb looked affronted. "I'm not that stupid."

"How could I possibly imagine you were?" Shaun said, his irony lost on Jeb. "Are you telling me Vince left the desk unlocked?"

"No," Jeb said. "You can pick that lock with a credit card, I bet."

Shaun acknowledged it was true. He could have done it himself in a few seconds. "I should have had a safe installed. A detail I won't overlook again. But I'm holding you responsible for your carelessness,

67

Jeb. I want you to find your friend and bring both her and my twenty grand back to me."

Jeb shifted from foot to foot. "She could be a thousand miles away by now," he protested.

"I don't care." Shaun's patience was almost exhausted. "Find her. You need me more than I need you. Don't forget it." He let menace creep into his voice, looked balefully into Jeb's eyes. The younger man didn't blink, but Shaun wasn't hoodwinked. While Jeb might be enough of a fool or psychopath to show no fear, he should have no doubt: one way or another, he'd be bringing Shaun twenty thousand pounds. If he didn't, he'd face the consequences.

Chapter 12 Charles

Two decades of commuting into the City had turned Charles into an early riser. At six, he took a tray into the bedroom with an espresso for himself and a pot of green tea for Deirdre.

"Thank you, darling." She yawned and stretched, throwing off the white silk covers to reveal her splendidly toned body. It had been another warm night and she was completely naked.

"I'm tempted to come back to bed," Charles observed, desire gripping him.

"Give into temptation, then," Deirdre said. "I always do." She sat up and leaned forward, pulling the loosely tied belt of his bathrobe. The garment immediately fell away from his body, revealing his erection. Deirdre licked it. "You like that, don't you, Chas?"

"Yes." Every nerve in his body suddenly felt alive. He stroked her hair, shoulders and breasts, squeezing her nipples, then slowly pushed her away, down onto the bed. Straddling her, he parted her legs and slipped inside.

Deirdre gasped with pleasure, moving her legs back and then stretching them to twist her feet around his neck. He was pulled further within. Deirdre practised yoga daily and the effect on her suppleness was evident. Eager to reciprocate, Charles kissed her lips tenderly and concentrated on her gratification.

His iPhone rang at six thirty. "Who the devil is that?" Charles grimaced. He let the phone default to voicemail.

"You'll have to pick it up, darling," Deirdre said, as the inevitable voicemail calls began.

"When we're done," Charles said, already aware the spell was broken. He brought Deirdre to a satisfactory, if unspectacular, climax before finishing himself.

69

His boss had left a message requesting an urgent call back. Cursing under his breath, as good manners precluded him from using bad language in front of a lady, Charles obliged.

"Yo, Charles. I didn't wake you up, did I?"

"No, Alex." Charles kept his tone friendly as ever. He didn't believe in bringing his emotions to work.

"Great stuff," Alex replied. "Can you get here within the hour? I want you to work on a new project, and we need to get our ducks in a row. You'll have to be NDAed by nine."

"All right, Alex. I'll leave now," Charles said, mentally clocking the unpaid overtime and resolving to leave early to compensate for it. He'd seen many of his colleagues succumb to stress over the years, and decided he wasn't going to join them. Since hitting forty, he'd refused to work for more than thirty five hours a week. Alex, ten years younger and doubtless destined for burnout, didn't see eye to eye with him on this. There was nothing he could do, though, in the face of Charles' charm, persistence and sheer ability. Charles was easily the most capable member of his team.

"Do you have to go so early, Chas?" Deirdre pulled a face.

"Sorry. The bank has another top secret project, and Alex wants me to sign a non-disclosure agreement."

"How annoying for you," she sympathised.

Charles had a quick blast in the shower, scraped his chin and dashed for the Tube. There was no time for breakfast, but at least he could enjoy a few minutes of blokey football chat with the smokers before his day started. This, and the buzz of solving IT problems that no one else could crack, ensured his work was congenial as long as there wasn't too much of it.

Alex either had no interest in football, or wasn't prepared to share it with Charles. Short and intense, he made an effort to chat to his superiors but avoided small talk with his team. As soon as he saw Charles walk into the cavernous, humming room where they both worked, he pointed to a break-out area. "Let's have a one to one," he said, handing Charles a sheaf of papers and a pen. "We need to find somewhere private."

Charles flicked through the papers as soon as they were seated, in a glass-walled booth which in reality was as private as a goldfish bowl. There was a non-disclosure letter for the new project, another letter saying his emails and phone calls would be monitored, and a notice forbidding him to buy or sell shares in several companies. One of them was Veritable Insurance, presumably because Amy worked there. He signed everything with a flourish, under Alex's impatient gaze.

"Thanks," Alex said. "Okay, Charles, I suppose you can guess what I'm going to ask you to do next."

Charles genuinely had no idea. He guessed some data was required for one of the redundancy exercises which the bank undertook, regular as clockwork, each year. All the staff who were culled seemed to be replaced within months, leading to a degree of cynicism amid his coterie of smokers. He decided silence was the best policy.

"You've signed the NDA for Project Termite," Alex said. "I want you to go to a meeting about it at nine, but meanwhile, I'll fill you in. You know of Veritable Insurance, of course." Here, Alex permitted himself a thin smile. "The CEO of Veritable is your girlfriend's brother, as we're both well aware. I therefore thought it inappropriate for you to work on this project, but I was overruled."

That was useful intelligence. Alex reported into the bank's Board. Charles had long suspected that he had supporters at that level, and here was the confirmation. He possessed friends in high places, and apparently, he had more than Alex. Wisely, he kept quiet.

"Bishopstoke Insurance is buying Veritable, and merging the two companies together. Both Boards have reached agreement and will recommend the deal to shareholders. We've been instructed by Bishopstoke to help them with the acquisition. We'll be arranging a rights issue for them."

"You mean," Charles said, eager to prove he understood what this involved, "Bishopstoke is asking its shareholders for cash, and needs

71

to prove the acquisition will be value for money. The bank will say it is, but we need to check that's actually the case first."

"Absolutely," Alex said. "Any questions?"

Charles was tempted to ask why the project was named after a destructive insect, but thought better of it. "What's my role in this?"

"Glad you asked," Alex said acerbically. "I want you to do a deep dive into Veritable's IT systems. We've got three days, so give it 110%."

"Ah, you mean a systems audit," Charles said. "That would normally take two weeks from start to finish, even with extra resources. I tell you what, lend me John and a couple of contractors, and I'll see what I can do. You'll have to arrange cover for our other tasks, though."

Alex's sallow face reddened. "I haven't got a budget for backfill."

"You're kidding," Charles said. "The bank's fee will be north of £10m. It always is." A subtle reminder that he had worked here far longer than Alex. "We can afford a few contractors, surely? If you won't give me time to do the job properly, there's no point asking me to do it. You'd better go to this meeting alone."

"I thought you could fit it in around your work. You always leave at five, so you've obviously got capacity."

"You shouldn't be putting me under stress and expecting me to do overtime at my age," Charles said, aware he had the upper hand. The Board wanted him to work on the project, so Alex would have to facilitate that or face awkward questions. Alex might decide to dispense with his services in future, of course. Charles had played the age card as a warning that he would expect a handsome redundancy package. He could walk into another job easily enough.

"I agree." Alex's demeanour suggested he did not. "I'll see you in the conference room at nine."

Charles had just enough time for a coffee and a smoke. He bumped into one of the directors, a fellow Crystal Palace supporter, in the street outside.

"Going to the Project Termite meeting?" his colleague asked, lighting a Marlboro.

Charles nodded.

"It'll be a cast of thousands. Don't stay too long. I'll make sure we're done with IT by ten, then you can go away and plan your audit. Bishopstoke has given us a stupid deadline. Just do your best."

"Is there a budget for it?" Charles asked.

"Of course. And enough left over for a big party afterwards."

It still took Charles the rest of his working day, and more, to plan the audit. The next day, he would be meeting Veritable's IT director in the morning. Much to his irritation, he ended up working past six o'clock.

He was supposed to attend a networking evening with Deirdre at the Institute of Directors, a gracious stucco building on Pall Mall. Having texted to say he would meet her there, he found his reception frosty.

"I can't believe you're late," she hissed. "You went to work stupidly early this morning."

"It was the project," Charles said.

"Oh, that." Deirdre appeared unimpressed.

He suspected she'd have been interested if she'd realised it involved Veritable, although he was far too professional to divulge it. If she ever found out he'd kept a secret like that, she'd be less than amused. "I don't know why you wanted me here anyway," he said.

"I won't get leched over if everyone sees I have a handsome, dashing boyfriend."

He preened, before Deirdre pointed out Camilla, the same bored-looking brunette he'd seen at their flat.

"Would you mind turning the charm on Camilla? I'm hoping to do some nutritional films with her."

Camilla, alas, did not smoke. She was a vegan and spent a good thirty minutes explaining the benefits of her diet, and the deficiencies of the Institute's canapés, to him.

"I thought they were rather yummy," Charles said, nibbling a smoked salmon blini.

"I don't eat anything with a face," Camilla said, scowling at Charles as if he were a cannibal.

"I can see you two are getting on famously," Deirdre said brightly, appearing like a particularly well-timed ray of sunlight.

"Well I'm feeling hungry listening to Camilla talking about her diet," Charles said, as Camilla shooed away the servers gliding past with trays of canapés. "In fact," he added desperately, "I'm rather tired. Why don't we go home soon and have supper at the flat?"

"Sounds like a plan," Deirdre agreed. "Would you like to join us, Camilla?"

"No thank you," the brunette sniffed, to Charles' relief. "I'm going back to Soho for a kale smoothie."

"I didn't realise that's what Soho was famous for," Charles observed when Camilla was out of earshot.

"Don't be too dismissive," Deirdre said. "She has her own TV programme already. Viewers love her. I suppose they think they'll be gorgeous too if they drink her smoothies. She looks like a young Elizabeth Taylor, doesn't she?"

"You're beautiful despite the complete absence of kale from your kitchen," Charles declared. He drew her towards him.

"You don't know all my guilty secrets," Deirdre said, holding his gaze just long enough for him to wonder.

"Then I'll make sure you eat properly tonight," Charles replied. "Supper in bed?"

He persuaded Deirdre to go ahead of him to the flat and popped into a Marks & Spencer food store nearby. Charles often went there; it was, as on this occasion, an excuse for a couple of cigarettes whilst appearing to be helpful. Back home, he rustled up rare steaks and salad, red wine in Deirdre's crystal glasses, profiteroles with chocolate sauce. He arranged the meal on a gilded tray they had bought together in Florence, and took it into the airy white bedroom. Deirdre was sitting up in bed, wearing a pink tulle baby doll nightdress.

"You look like Barbie," he laughed.

She giggled. "Well, Ken," she said, "show me what's for supper."

He left the tray next to her on the bedside table and pulled up a chair. Tenderly, he cut up a forkful of steak and fed it to her.

"Mmm." She mouthed appreciative noises.

They both ate the main course and pudding with relish. Charles approved of Deirdre's appetite. She exercised so much – it was her profession after all – that she could eat whatever she chose, with no need for the diets that seemed to turn his female colleagues into snappish dragons.

"Chas," Deirdre murmured greedily, "is that an extra pot of chocolate sauce?"

"It is," he admitted. "Shall we share it?" He was already removing his clothing, and with one swift stroke, he lifted away her flimsy nightdress. Dipping a finger in the sauce, he spread it over her lips and nipples, then turned his attention between her thighs. Gradually, he licked the chocolate from her skin.

Deirdre returned the favour, painting him with the sugary liquid, nibbling and licking him sensuously.

He could bear it no longer. He pulled her face to his and rewarded her with a deep French kiss. Then, at last, he began to make love; slowly, and without interruption. "I've waited all day for this," he gasped.

Deirdre's brown eyes shone. "I waited all my life," she said, "and it was worth it."

Chapter 13 Amy

Amy dialled 999.

"Emergency. Which service?" It was a woman's voice.

"Police."

"Putting you through."

The next speaker was a man. "Where are you?"

Amy gave her address.

"What is the emergency?"

"It's my flatmate – she's vanished." Amy's voice trembled.

"How old is she?"

"Twenty four."

"Does she have mental health issues; suicidal at all?"

"No."

"This number is for emergencies only, my dear. You need to call 101."

Amy was indignant. Why was a young woman's disappearance so unimportant? It was the first thing she asked when she rang the non-emergency line.

"She's an adult and free to come and go," the male operator explained. "Do you still want to report this?"

Amy said she did, and they went through all his scripted questions. "She wouldn't just go away for two days without telling me," Amy said, "and she'd reply to my texts." As she spoke the words, she asked herself if they were true. She had lodged in Fitzrovia for a mere two months. Did she really know Kat? They had shared late night wine and laughter, sipped coffee together to ward off weekend hangovers, partied at the glamorous events to which Kat somehow secured invitations. Despite that, Kat had told her very little about herself. Her childhood and family were almost a closed book. An aunt in Birmingham had been mentioned in passing, as had a father in the drinks trade. Even Jeb, who had visited the flat most weeks to take Kat out for cocktails, was a man of mystery.

She finished the call and was given an incident number. "You need to quote that to the police," she was told. The operator gave no assurances that the police would be in touch. In the circumstances, Amy was relieved when they visited next morning, although she would have preferred not to be woken at six.

The doorbell, strident as a siren, wormed its way into her dream until it could no longer be ignored. There was a spyhole in the front door through which she noted the uniformed man and woman. She opened the door.

"Miss Amy Satterthwaite?"

"Yes."

Once they'd introduced themselves as PCs James Burnett and Saffron Cole from the local police station, Amy ushered them inside, to Kat's room. Here, the visitors could sit on Kat's sofa bed and she on one of the two folding dining chairs. In Amy's bedroom, by contrast, there was barely clearance to walk past her single bed, and no seating save the bed itself. "This is Kat's room," she explained.

"Kat would be your flatmate?" PC Cole asked. "Does Bronwen Jones live here too?"

"Bronwen moved out two months ago, when I moved in. It's just Kat and me."

"Where's Kat at the moment?" Cole wanted to know.

"You tell me." This was quite extraordinary. Amy had reported Kat as missing. Didn't they understand that? She hadn't even mentioned Bronwen, and why should she when they'd never met? "Wait," Amy said, "I'll fetch the incident number. I have it written down in my room." She would make them tea as well. That was what witnesses did for the police in crime dramas, wasn't it? Perhaps they would prefer coffee; she must ask.

The two officers exchanged glances. "I'll come with you," Cole said.

"Good. You can help me carry the tea." Amy's brain really wasn't functioning well. She was used to rising half an hour later, which in itself was early enough.

They walked through the narrow corridor together, stopping briefly for Amy to open the door of the kitchenette and switch on the kettle. "What would you prefer – tea or coffee?" she asked.

"Tea for me and a coffee for Jamie, both white," Cole replied.

Amy left the kettle to boil, and obtained the scribbled-down number from her room.

"It's cosy in here, isn't it?" Cole said, her eyes on the small, barely accessible window a metre above the bedhead. For the first time, she smiled at Amy. "Shall I help you make the drinks? Jamie just takes a spot of milk in his. I know exactly how he likes it."

Amy put two teaspoons of instant coffee in her own mug. She saw that Cole had noticed, although the other woman remained silent. Obviously, the police were trained to spot every detail. "Please help yourself," she said, placing mugs, teabags, coffee and milk in front of the officer.

They took the drinks into Kat's room. Amy unfolded the small black dining table. "Now," she said, "What do you need from me? I'll tell you everything you want to know."

"Thank you," PC Burnett said. He took a photograph from his pocket. "Do you recognise this man?"

It was a dark-skinned young man of south Asian appearance, perhaps from India but more likely one of the millions of Englishmen whose parents and grandparents had emigrated from the subcontinent. "No," Amy said.

"That's strange," Cole said, "because you married him a fortnight ago."

Amy felt giddy. The world blurred before her eyes. She clutched at her seat, willing herself to stay upright. "That's impossible," she said. "I've never been married. I don't even have a boyfriend."

78

"This is Ahmed Khan," Burnett said. "He came to London from Bangladesh on a student visa, to learn English. That's quite common. The majority of students complete their studies and go home. Ahmed didn't. He had a job as a chef. Whether he was a diligent student too, I don't know. Most visa over-stayers learn enough English to tell me to F myself. I haven't spoken to Ahmed himself – yet – but his boss tells me Ahmed was deeply in love with you and decided to stay in London to marry you. The records of St Edyth's church in the East End show that he did so this year on July the first. The vicar's confirmed it. He remembers you well. After all, you and Ahmed went to marriage classes at which he presided before the happy day."

"Perhaps it was another Amy Satterthwaite?"

"With the same address?" Burnett said warily.

"We are investigating this, and a number of other weddings at St Edyth's," Cole said. "We suspect they're sham marriages and criminal offences have been committed. We'd like you to come to the station to make a statement."

Amy took a deep breath. Suspicion was growing within her; the fear that her flatmate and friend had stolen her identity to marry Ahmed Khan. It all made sense: Kat's intense interest in Amy's background, borrowing her passport and birth certificate to 'show the landlord', even Kat's cheerful admission that she was about to make a short-term marriage. Had that been on the first of July? Amy struggled to remember.

"Are you all right?" Cole asked, her voice sympathetic.

"Not really," Amy said, tears beginning to well. "This is all tied in with Kat's disappearance, isn't it? She's stolen my identity to marry this man, Ahmed Khan. Why would she do that?"

Burnett rubbed a thumb and forefinger together. "Money," he said. "The Ahmeds of this world believe they'll have the right to remain in the UK if they marry a British citizen. They'll pay handsomely for that."

"We can't really comment until we've checked our records on your flatmate," Cole said, soothingly. "Listen, you gave us the reference number, so Jamie and I will read the incident report back at the station. We'll be in touch to arrange for you to see us there to make your statement." She turned to her colleague. "I don't think we need to ask her to do that straight away."

"Are you sure?" Burnett was more sceptical.

"I'm thinking about the descriptions we were given," Cole said cryptically.

"Fine," he shrugged. "We'll be leaving in a moment, then. Before we go, do you have a forwarding address for Bronwen Jones, by any chance?"

"No." Amy struggled to recall whether she even knew where Bronwen worked, or why she'd moved. Kat hadn't said a great deal about her.

"Please tell us if you find one," Burnett said. "Thanks for the coffee, by the way. Absolutely perfect."

Cole winked at Amy. "I've given you our telephone numbers. Just ring if you have any questions, all right? Or if you come across any information about Bronwen."

Once they'd left, Amy hit the speed dial on her phone. Her call to Kat went straight to voicemail, as had all the others she'd made in the past forty eight hours. She sent a text, with little hope of a reply, and began to get ready for work.

Chapter 14 Ross

Ross clutched his head. A hangover throbbed at his temples, a reminder of a wild night at Diamonds with his friends. After he cleaned up at blackjack, it had been champagne all round.

The coffee machine was broken again. Ross shook it – the percussive approach to maintenance occasionally worked – and tutted. He was tempted to buy another for the office out of his own pocket, but then he would have to email a helpdesk in India to ask for it to be PAT tested. Simone, the secretary who was supposed to handle the team's admin, had simply said she couldn't touch that sort of thing; such support services were outsourced now, and it was far too complicated. He suspected she was cross because he'd shouted at her last week. She was in the wrong job. Anyone who didn't understand the importance of his work, or the contribution made by strong coffee, shouldn't be a PA in the City.

It was on his fourth trip to the machine at the other end of the office that the dreary girl caught his eye. He remembered then that she was Kat's flatmate. What was she called? He couldn't think of it for the life of him, but fortunately, each workstation had a nameplate placed prominently above it. 'Amy Satterthwaite', he read.

Ross strolled over to her. "Oy, Satterthwaite," he said in a Mockney accent.

She looked him up and down with evident dislike. "Stop taking the mickey, Ross," she said.

"What have I done wrong?" he asked, pretending innocence.

The slim Asian girl next to Amy, whose workstation announced her as Parveen Patel, said, "I hope you've got a good reason to bother a member of my team. We're up against a tight deadline this afternoon."

"I was going to ask after Amy's flatmate," he protested.

"There's a time and a place for that," Parveen said, "and it isn't at work." Her steely gaze told him not to argue.

Armed with Amy's full name, he could send a message to her from his PC, and he did so as soon as he returned to his desk.

'Sorry I made a poor joke,' he wrote. He wasn't sorry at all, but she obviously had no sense of humour. A brief apology might persuade her to help him. 'Can you ask Kat to call me, please?'

Her reply was swift. 'You'll be lucky.'

'Please,' he responded. 'I didn't see her at Diamonds last night. They said she should have been there but wasn't. I'm worried about her.'

He was even more concerned when he saw what she wrote next. 'Me too. She's vanished. She hasn't answered my calls or emails either.'

'Can I see you after work?' he wrote.

'Didn't you listen to Parveen? We're working till the witching hour.'

'Lunch tomorrow?'

She wrote: 'Rustica. 1pm. You're paying.'

Chapter 15 Amy

It wasn't quite midnight when Amy arrived home. It had been another late night at the office though, fuelled with pizzas and black coffee. This time, Parveen had paid for a taxi.

She had to walk through the underground car park to reach her flat. Usually, it was bright with fluorescent strip lights. Just for once, they weren't lit. She switched on her smartphone's rather underpowered flashlight. It gave enough illumination to find her keys and start unlocking the front door.

If she hadn't been so fatigued, so relieved to be home at last, she might have noticed the man lurking in the shadows by the gym. As it was, her first indication of his presence was his hand on her shoulder and cold metal at her throat.

"Hello, Kat," he whispered conversationally, "Don't scream or I'll spoil that pretty face of yours."

Amy froze, unable even to speak, to say she wasn't Kat. She didn't know what was going to happen next, but could guess it wasn't pleasant.

"Open the door." He pronounced it dough-ah, as Jeb might have done, but she knew instinctively it wasn't Jeb. Nor was it the mysterious, well-spoken stranger who'd searched Kat's bedroom and walked out with two sorry shrubs. He had keys anyway; he'd have no need to ambush her in the car park.

She turned first one key, then the other. Her attacker pushed her against the door, so it opened and she stumbled inside. All the while, he was careful to keep the knife pressed against her throat. She assumed, at any rate, that it was a knife.

"Put the light on," he said, as soon as they were both inside. She fumbled for the switch. It was hard to find; she was trembling so much. Meanwhile, he removed the hand from her shoulder, using it to close the door behind them. She heard a gentle thud and felt a slight gust of air as he did so.

Light flooded the flat's mean corridor. She heard him gasp and curse.

"Who are you?" he breathed.

"I should ask you that." Amy's voice shook.

"No." His tone was menacing. "I ask the questions, okay? And I want to know your name." He took the blade away from her neck and she saw it flash, towards the right hand edge of her field of vision, as he flicked it closed. He spun her around to face him, a tall dark-haired man in his forties. Older women, her mother for instance, might even have found him good-looking when his blue eyes were laughing. Now, they were angry, wary. "Not a sister, obviously. Flatmate?"

"Yes. I'm Amy."

"Are there any more of you? Expecting anyone else back here tonight?"

She seized her chance. "Yes, my boyfriend – any minute now." To her dismay, she sounded dreadfully unconvincing.

"Boyfriend?" He took a long look at her. "No, I don't think so," he said slowly. "But just in case, you're going to bolt that door. And if he rings, you'll tell him to go away." He drew a finger across his neck. "Or else. Now, we're going to sit down and get to know each other. In here, I think." He opened the door to Kat's room and shoved her inside.

It was obvious that Kat still hadn't returned. The glow from the corridor showed Amy that nothing had changed since the morning. She flicked the light switch, shrinking from her attacker.

His eyes flashed, his mouth twitching at the corners. Nothing escaped his sight, she realised. He was as vigilant as the policemen had been, yet clearly not on the side of law and order.

"Give me answers and you won't get hurt," the knifeman said, his words hanging heavy in the hot, still air. "No lies, no flirting. Just tell it straight."

It was a reprieve of sorts, and she felt a flood of relief despite his contempt. She couldn't imagine flirting with someone her father's age. Then, she remembered January's dalliance with Ali's uncle, and shivered.

For the second time that day, she sat in one of Kat's uncomfortable folding chairs. Whatever he'd just said, she didn't want to be next to him on the sofa. "What do you want?" she asked.

"Where's Kat? I need to see her."

"I don't know."

He took the knife from his pocket.

"No," Amy said, "I really don't know. If I did, I'd tell you. She's been gone for three days and I can't reach her. I've tried, believe me." This was no time for heroics. Had she the slightest idea of Kat's whereabouts, she would have divulged them, of that she was sure.

His eyes darted down to the knife. He flicked it open, stroked its blade, then looked up at her again. "I need answers, Amy," he said, almost sorrowfully. "If someone had stolen twenty grand from you, you'd want some answers too."

"Kat stole twenty thousand pounds?" A week ago she wouldn't have believed it. Now, she couldn't be sure. "That's not all she's done. She married an illegal immigrant, using my name. The police were round this morning."

"Do they know where she is?"

Amy sighed. "No."

"Good. I want to see her before the police do. I don't suppose they've searched this flat for clues to her whereabouts?"

She was silent.

"No," he said. "I thought not. You and me, Amy, we're going to do that now, before any such clues might do a vanishing act like our mutual friend. Show me Kat's room."

"You're in it."

He looked around, shook his head. "Really? I thought this was the lounge. Okay, I want you to take everything out of those boxes." He

85

pointed to a stack of wooden wine crates, painted white, in which Kat's belongings were stowed.

The top crate was crammed with shopping bags, over a dozen of them, bearing the names of designer boutiques: Prada, Marc Jacobs, Miu Miu and more. Reluctantly, Amy picked up a bag.

"Open it," the knifeman said.

It was from Agent Provocateur, a powder pink paper bag sealed with a black ribbon. Carefully, Amy untied the bow. Inside, there was a pink cardboard box.

"Now that," he ordered.

"Must I?" Amy pleaded. "These are Kat's personal things."

"That's the whole point."

Silently, she opened the box, unfolded the black tissue paper inside and shook out a frilly silk underwear set. A receipt showed it had cost two hundred pounds.

He whistled, leering. "Very nice. Now the rest."

Altogether, Kat had spent over four thousand pounds on unworn purchases. "A shopping addiction," he said thoughtfully, reflecting Amy's surprised reaction. "Carry on."

The crates below mostly contained clothes, neatly folded, and shoes in bags. There were a few books, overspill from the shelves by the wall, and finally, a box file containing paperwork.

"Give me that," the dangerous stranger commanded. He fished out a letter. "Dearest Kat," he read aloud, "I hope you are well. I am fine, and so is Cedric the Cat, but he is very old now. I have a little job now at Treasures in Harborne. Same old, same old. Do write and tell me your news. With love, Auntie Lizzie." He paused. "Isn't that sweet?" he said sarcastically. "Let's see if there's more of the same."

He rifled through the box, shaking his head. Evidently, nothing further was deemed worthy of comment. He asked her to empty the only other article of storage in the room, a large rosewood chest, but that merely yielded towels and bedding.

"Interesting, and predictable," he muttered. "I'll tell you what we haven't found. No suitcase, money, passport, women's things like cosmetics. No certificates for qualifications, birth, marriage even." He looked pointedly at Amy. "She's done a runner."

Amy bit her tongue. He was unlikely to appreciate being told he was stating the obvious.

He pocketed the letter. "I'll be back. And you'll tell me where she is, okay?" He fingered the knife again. "Not a word to the Old Bill. I've never been here, not on your life."

"What about the CCTV?" she couldn't resist challenging him.

"What about it?" he said dismissively. "None in that car park. I cut the wires." He stood to leave, putting a finger to his lips. "You're a lucky, lucky girl, Amy, because I believe you. Thousands wouldn't. Now don't forget – not a dicky bird, okay?"

When he'd gone, Amy bolted the door and searched the kitchenette for alcohol. Finding a bottle of Snow Mountain vodka, less than a quarter full, she drank all that was left of it and went straight to bed.

The next morning, Amy slept through her alarm. Bleary-eyed, she dry-shampooed her hair and crawled into work at ten. She expected sharp words from Parveen, but none were forthcoming until she switched off her computer and picked up her handbag at five to one.

"I thought you'd be working through lunch after that late start," Parveen said.

"I have a prior engagement," Amy said grandly.

Parveen rolled her eyes. "Well, you'd better make up the time later." There was no point reminding her they'd left after eleven the night before.

Rustica was right next to the Thames, a new wine bar serving tapas. Amy had looked at the price list outside when it opened, and dismissed it as far above her budget. Sometimes she felt like a Victorian orphan, nose pressed against the windows of London's pleasure palaces. When she'd complained to her father about it, he'd laughed and said that was why he climbed the greasy pole.

Ross was clearly far enough up the greasy pole that the prices at Rustica were small change for him. He ordered a series of expensive dishes, but no wine.

"A large dry white for me," Amy said. Despite her hangover and the nightmarish quality of her encounter with the knifeman, she retained sharp images of his scorn and the fear he invoked. Wine would blur the edges.

He raised an eyebrow. "I never drink at lunchtime."

"Well, you should," she said. "It'll help you get through the afternoon at Boredom Central." They were bold words, and she regretted them when he looked pointedly at her handbag, as if expecting to see a bottle of vodka in it. She decided to order the costliest dessert on the menu later to punish him.

"How come Kat shares a flat with you?" Ross asked, with just the slightest edge of contempt.

In truth, Amy had wondered about that when Kat had first asked. She had a pretty shrewd idea now. Kat could have been attracted by her sparkling personality, but more likely had seen her as someone who could be easily married, in name anyway. "We met at a party," she said. "I was looking for somewhere central to live and she had a room. And you're one of the gamblers at Diamonds, aren't you? I bet that impresses your boss."

Ross didn't rise to the bait. "Actually, there are a few of us who like a night out there," he said. "We set ourselves a limit; perhaps a hundred pounds or so."

Amy gawped at him.

"I expect to lose it," Ross said. "I know the odds are against me. I've had some big wins on blackjack, though."

It was always the same, Amy thought sourly. You had to start with a lot of money in order to make any more.

Ross continued. "Kat was always friendly, chatty, kind, even though we weren't high rollers. I think we stopped her getting bored when it was quiet."

That was unlikely, Amy thought, but kept the words to herself.

"I really liked her."

Yes, the way that all the guys did, Amy thought. "Why her?" she asked. There were any number of pretty girls working at the casino, some of them rather more flexible in their moral outlook.

"She's so different from everyone I know."

"No kidding," Amy said. "Let me guess – you've got a maths degree."

He nodded.

"Who did you hang out with at uni?"

"People on my course. And the Maths Soc."

"And now?"

"Colleagues. Actuaries."

"So, you're hardly exposing yourself to a broad range of people, are you?"

Ross forced a grin. "No, I suppose not."

"What do you actuaries do all day?" she asked him, half curious and half dreading the tedium of the answer that would follow. She wasn't disappointed.

"The company depends on us. We price risk," Ross replied.

She saw he found her blank expression less than endearing. It wasn't fair. Kat would have looked like that too, and he would have thought her charming. Then again, he fancied Kat and not Amy. She decided that was just as well; he was so annoying.

"Come on," Ross said, "don't tell me you've no idea what a profit and loss account is?"

"Er, sort of." There had been an accountancy module in her marketing degree, but she rarely turned up to the lectures. Had she scraped through that one or failed it? She recalled very little.

University had been one long party. Working for Parveen, on the other hand, was the hangover.

"We won't pay you overtime. We don't expect you to work any," she'd been told. That was so far removed from reality, it was beyond a joke. Worse, her parents didn't have a clue. They thought all she had to do was turn up at nine and work hard until five o'clock. They didn't realise she stayed late into the evening, with a little weekend homework for pudding. Their lives weren't like this. She remembered dinner on the table for Charles at 6.30pm throughout her childhood. He would have had to leave work promptly for that. Rachel merely dabbled at part-time jobs, occasionally attending office parties with Charles and making sure to tell his bosses they were underpaying him. As for Deirdre, one shake of her tanned limbs and punters flocked to download her videos. If she hadn't rushed to sink her claws into Charles, he would surely have patched up his marriage with Rachel.

Life was too complicated. Amy wished her parents were together again, united in their support for her, not scurrying into the arms of new lovers when their daughter couldn't even find a satisfactory boyfriend.

"Anyway," Amy said, aware from Ross' expression that disillusionment was written on her face, "I really need to find Kat and I'm going to start looking for her." Whatever Kat had done, she deserved to be warned about the men who were hunting her, especially the sinister knifeman. Perhaps, if she saved Kat's life, Kat would admit the sham marriage to the police. She sighed. "I don't suppose you can help? Parveen's told me I can't have any time off until September, and I guess you're the same."

"Why don't you take sick leave?" Ross said. "And you're wrong about my holidays. I've got as much time as I need. I'm about to take a six month sabbatical, beginning tonight. We're allowed to after ten years."

Amy stared at him, slightly startled that Ross would suggest sick leave. The fact that he'd endured the dullness of Veritable for a full decade simply proved how stuffy he was.

"I just thought I'd never done anything really exciting in my life. I wanted to travel. I bought two tickets to Thailand. Kat and I got on so well, I planned to ask her to come with me."

Kat might have done, Amy supposed, if only to spend two weeks in a luxury hotel before she succumbed to boredom and flew back.

As if he had glimpsed her thoughts, he said, "I bought flexible tickets," adding, "That means I needn't travel straight away. I'll find Kat first. Any idea where to start?"

A waitress asked if they wanted more wine. Framed by his spectacles, Ross' sky-blue eyes showed his disapproval. The sight called to mind her recent visitor's chilly, implacable gaze. Amy shuddered and ordered another glass.

"I thought that was you." Deirdre's husky voice sounded behind her. "Chas, look who's here."

Amy turned to see her father and his paramour, bright-eyed and holding hands. It was embarrassing at their age, but they appeared utterly shameless.

"Aren't you going to introduce us to your friend?" Charles asked.

Grudgingly, Amy said, "Ross, meet Charles and Deirdre."

Ross looked up fleetingly, then rose to his feet. He'd obviously decided it was worth acknowledging the couple. Amy wasn't surprised. Charles' wardrobe, now Deirdre was paying for it, signalled money: Savile Row suits, crisp cotton shirts, Italian silk ties. Deirdre herself was glamorous as ever, wearing a short, tight red dress which displayed her toned figure perfectly. Her crimson lips revealed dazzling white teeth. Ross was visibly impressed. He offered his hand.

"Call me Dee," Deirdre said, leaning forward to shake his hand whilst artfully flaunting her generous bosom.

"I'm Amy's father," Charles said. "And this is my partner, Dee. Tell me about yourself, Ross."

"Ross and I are colleagues," Amy interrupted.

"Oh yes?" Charles said. "What line are you in, Ross?"

"I'm an actuary."

"A shrewd choice of career," Charles opined. "I imagine your earning potential is above average even for the City of London."

"I'm sure it is," Ross said, clearly enjoying having his ego stroked.

"You must be very clever," Deirdre said.

"A first in maths, and first time passes in the actuarial exams," Ross boasted.

"Listen," Amy said crossly, "Ross and I were trying to have a private conversation."

"Well, we mustn't stop you," Charles said. He shook Ross' hand in parting. "Good to meet you." He shepherded Deirdre to another table. They laughed and chatted together, with the odd sidelong glance at Amy.

They clearly thought Amy and Ross were on a date. Amy considered whether to admit the truth, or even to mention it to Ross. He would, no doubt, be horrified at the thought. She decided to let sleeping dogs lie.

That wasn't all she would withhold from Ross. If she so much as hinted Deirdre was David Saxton's sister, Ross was likely to be obsequious to the point of servility. Worse, he might tell their colleagues. The embarrassment would be unbearable. Nor, for different reasons, would she mention Kat's mysterious visitors, or even Jeb, who might or might not be Kat's boyfriend, might or might not be a gangster. Ross seemed to want to help her find Kat; she didn't want to deter him by suggesting the search would be perilous or pointless.

"You asked where to start," she said.

"Yes," he said, and then made a surprisingly sensible comment. "People do disappear in London of course, taking advantage of the anonymity of the city. But if I lived here, I'd go somewhere else. Kat's Facebook page says she comes from Birmingham."

"Well, she won't be difficult to find then," Amy said acidly, unwilling to give him credit for the germ of a good idea. "A mere million people live there, so how hard can it be?"

"Where else do you suggest?"

"She has a relative in Harborne, wherever that is. Auntie Lizzie. She works in a place called Treasures."

92

"Let me google that." Ross reached for his smartphone. "Harborne is in Birmingham, you silly girl. I was right all along."

"Sorry," Amy said with bad grace, smarting at being labelled a silly girl. "We'd better go there first, then. As long as you're paying. I can barely afford to travel on the Tube."

Ross agreed without batting an eyelid, then asked for the bill. As they walked away from Rustica, he said with a backward glance at the river, "Do you think we'll find her? I fear she may be at the bottom of the Thames."

"I believe she's alive. She took her suitcase, after all," Amy said. Rainclouds were gathering. Despite her reassurances to Ross, she shivered in apprehension of the coming storm. They weren't the only ones heading for Harborne.

Chapter 16 Ross

As soon as Cari summoned Ross, he was glad he hadn't indulged in a lunchtime drink. It was vital to keep his wits about him when he saw her. She was sharp as a razor, and nowhere near as forgiving. Like him, she had a first in Maths. In her case, if the university had been capable of awarding an even higher class of undergraduate degree, it would surely have done so. All his life, he'd been used to interacting with people far less intelligent than him. Cari made him feel uncomfortable.

Spending time in her office set him on edge too, for Ross coveted it. Although a small room, it was hers alone, and it had a much-prized view of the Thames. As he entered, he looked across to the Tate Modern on the South Bank, beyond which the Shard cut through low rainclouds like a knife.

A stray sunray caught Cari's short red hair, appearing to set it on fire. Coupled with her thin frame and cream linen dress, the effect was of a flaming match, or stick of dynamite about to blow.

She didn't waste any time. "We're going to merge with Bishopstoke."

Ross whistled. Rumours of a merger with Bishopstoke had persisted in the City for several months. "That's great news," he said.

She fixed him with a gimlet gaze. "Of course, you know that means you can't take a sabbatical."

"But you signed it off," he protested. "So did HR. Even Davey Saxton."

"That was then. This is now," Cari snapped. "You can't expect a long term career here if you're not serious about it."

Why did they ever put women into positions of power? His father had often opined on the subject, at length. He was turning into his father, he mused, and he wasn't ashamed of it. "It was signed off," he repeated.

94

Cari glared. "I'm not reaching you, am I? You have no emotional intelligence, that's your trouble. I'm referring this to Davey."

He would like to hear her tell David Saxton about it. Despite her stratospheric IQ, she had all the empathy of Attila the Hun.

In the event, David Saxton passed by his desk later, clapped him on the shoulder, and said he hoped he'd enjoy his break. "No one's indispensable, not even me," Saxton guffawed.

Ross suspected David Saxton meant the former at least, if not the latter. Saxton must believe himself totally necessary to the company's success; how else could he justify a salary in line with a competent Premier League footballer's wages? Ross reflected bitterly that a footballer was a great deal more entertaining. He comforted himself with the thought that he would have Saxton's job one day.

Chapter 17 Jeb

Jeb was woken by a phone call. "I'm waiting outside," Shaun said curtly.

Cursing, Jeb looked at the time. He'd suggested to Shaun that nine o'clock was far too early, but his boss was having none of it. Pulling on designer jeans, T-shirt and trainers, he finished the ensemble with a leather jacket. Last night's washing-up lay festering in the sink as he lit a cigarette and left his flat.

"Shall I drive, boss?" he asked, looking covetously at Shaun's top-of-the-range Mercedes. Jeb wasn't insured to take the wheel; in fact no one was, but that had never bothered them. The Merc, with its cloned number plate, slipped gloriously under the DVLA's radar.

"Later, if I have a drink," Shaun snapped. He, too, was evidently grumpy about the early start. At the first petrol station on the A12, he insisted on stopping to buy coffee.

"I'll have a little pick-me-up with it," Jeb said, swallowing a couple of amphetamine tablets. "Want any?"

"Sure." Shaun accepted them gratefully.

"You know where we're going?" Jeb asked.

"Some northern slagheap in Birmingham. I've programmed the satnav," Shaun said.

"The last and only time I went there, it was with West Ham. We lost. I never went back," Jeb said. He had enjoyed a gratifying fight, however, and smirked at the recollection. His own group of lads had outnumbered the Villa fans they decided to tackle, and made doubly sure of avenging their team's honour by employing knives.

"They just don't play right, those Birmingham clubs," Shaun observed. "We need more Academy football in the league."

"Even West Ham don't play Academy style any more," Jeb said, repeating a view he had already stated ad nauseam in the White Horse, and indeed, to Shaun.

"True," Shaun conceded. As they hit the M25, his spirits appeared to be rising. Even the traffic management system and roadworks failed to dent his bonhomie. The caffeine and speed were doing their job. The conversation shifted amicably to boxing and darts as they sped up the M1.

Chapter 18 Amy

Amy coughed. "I have a terrible sore throat, and a headache. I was up three times in the night with vomiting and diarrhoea."

Parveen, on the other end of the line, was silent.

"And I've got dreadful stomach cramps," Amy continued.

"You'd better stay at home then," Parveen said eventually. "Don't forget to complete a sick form when you're back. And email me when you feel up to doing some work at home. I've got six reports for you to write."

"Quite finished?" Ross said icily when she ended the call. "When you throw a sickie, it's advisable to limit your symptoms to one or two, so you can ring the changes. What are you going to tell her next time – that you've broken your arm?"

"Are you ready to walk to Euston?" Amy asked, changing the subject.

"I'm ready to walk to the cab rank round the corner," Ross said, gesturing to their overnight bags.

They left her flat. He had insisted on meeting her there, and after a few remarks about the size of the flat, had conducted a cursory search of Kat's room. Amy suspected it was so he could finger the silk and lace underwear folded in one of the wine crates. As she anticipated, he'd found nothing she hadn't already under the knifeman's baleful gaze.

Ross bought first class rail tickets at Euston. Standard class was clearly beneath his dignity. As well as the extra space, there was the welcome and wholly unexpected bonus of a free breakfast on the train. Ross ordered a full English, then began reading the Financial Times. His pink broadsheet divided the table like a wall between them.

"Do you have to read that?" Amy asked, as she tucked into her croissants and coffee.

Ross peered over the edge of his newspaper. "You're right," he said. "I could be doing this online." He retrieved an iPad from his bag and started tapping away at it, occasionally stopping to sip coffee. The cooked breakfast arrived and he ate it with relish. "I'll work this off later," he explained. "I've booked a hotel with a gym."

"Separate rooms, I hope?" Amy said.

Ross spluttered into his coffee. "Certainly. You shouldn't need to ask. And before I hear your next question, I've booked for one night only. It won't take long to find the aunt, meet Kat, make sure she's got her passport with her and whisk her away to Thailand."

He was so arrogant, Amy longed to slap him. Resisting temptation, she decided instead to give him a dose of his own medicine. Fishing a paperback from her handbag, she inserted earphones and began listening to Beyoncé.

Ross finished his breakfast quickly and returned to his iPad. The train had just left Birmingham International station when he nudged her.

"What?" Amy had started to doze off. She had a sleep deficit to make good.

Ross was looking pleased with himself again. "I've just been playing online poker. I won back the cost of our train fares and hotel."

"How?"

"It's all about maths," Ross explained, adding cuttingly, "Kat would understand."

"Well done," Amy said grudgingly. "Remind me never to play poker against anyone, especially not an actuary, and most of all, not you."

Birmingham New Street was the next stop, a warren of white tunnels, silvery escalators and sliding doors. "For crying out loud," Ross grumbled as they stood on the escalator.

"What's the problem?" Amy was puzzled.

"Nobody's moving." Although in London, there would have been two lines of people, those on the left racing past the stationary passengers on the right, here everyone stood still.

"It's not the Tube, Ross," Amy said, suppressing a grin.

Still impatient, Ross insisted they took a taxi from the station.

"Are you sure?" the driver asked when Ross barked the name of their hotel. "It isn't far."

"Just drive there," Ross said, in his usual imperious manner.

The driver looked sympathetically at Amy, and shrugged. Three minutes later, he delivered them to the Malmaison hotel, a few hundred metres away from the station.

"We could have walked," Amy muttered.

Ross ignored her. He strode into the polished wood lobby as if he owned the hotel. A discussion followed about the readiness of the rooms, concluding with Ross thanking the reception staff for their upgrade.

Amy's mounting irritation was quelled by the luxurious hotel. They were allocated adjacent suites. Amy's, a vision in caramel and cream, was large enough to swallow her London flat whole, with room for the tiny gym besides. The Malmaison itself boasted both a gym and spa. Ross told her curtly that she could try them later. Once he'd dropped his bags, he was impatient to take a cab to Harborne.

Used to long commutes between central London and its suburbs, Amy was pleasantly surprised when the taxi drew to a halt after ten minutes. Treasures turned out to be a gift shop sandwiched between a hairdresser and an estate agent.

"I think you should buy something," Amy hissed as they entered the shop, concerned that Ross' rudeness might close the only line of enquiry they had. "To get them on our side."

"All right," he agreed. "Choose some jewellery for Kat. You know what she likes."

There was a glittery selection of earrings inside a glass display cabinet. Amy selected long silver spirals and took them to the till. "My friend will pay," she said.

The woman at the till, a bleached blonde perhaps ten years older, laughed. "That's what boyfriends are for, isn't it?"

Amy squeezed Ross' forearm, hoping he'd play along. "Oh yes," she said. "By the way, we came here because we thought someone called Lizzie worked here. My flatmate in London wanted us to give regards."

"What a coincidence," the saleswoman said. "Two gentlemen came looking for Liz Clements only an hour ago. They were from London too. You could tell from the accent."

Were the plant lover and knifeman working together? Amy sneaked a glance at Ross.

His face was a picture. "I wonder who..."

"I've no idea," she deadpanned.

"I told them she'd be in at five," the blonde declared. "She's our cleaner. I suppose they'll be back then. They said they were going to the pub."

It was barely noon. They had several hours to wait and the prospect of an overcrowded meeting after that. "I wish we could see her now," Amy said. "We'll have to go back to London soon. It would be such a shame to miss her."

It was Ross who clinched it. Rearranging his features into a boyish grin, he appealed, "Do you think we could have her address, please? I thought she'd be here now. Five is too late for us." He patted Amy's hand. "Why don't you find some earrings for yourself, dear?"

Amy saw the blonde's face soften. They came away with an address: a tower block, which they were assured was easy to find, in a backstreet a stone's throw from the shops.

"Thanks for the earrings," Amy said, as they left Treasures. "Dear." She fingered her ears, where his purchase dangled; tribal-inspired turquoise stones hanging from silver chains.

At last, Ross was happy to walk. The suburban streets were a cheerful mix of red brick villas and grander, detached houses, each different from the last. It was a setting in which the obviously council-owned towers looked wholly out of place. Lizzie's block was the nearest of four; all soaring white structures, reflecting blue skies in a grid of windows.

Amy punched Lizzie's number into the door buzzer. "We've been sent by Linda Sweetman from Treasures," she explained.

Lizzie buzzed them in. "Linda phoned ahead," she said. "I'm on the ninth floor. Should I switch on my kettle?"

The apartment's bright red door had its own bell too. It was opened so swiftly they were sure Lizzie had been waiting behind it. She was plump, short and middle-aged. Her hair, snow-white and bobbed, was a plain foil to a heavily made-up face. Her pink lipsticked mouth broke into a smile as she opened the door. "Why's Linda sending me visitors, then?" she asked.

"We had to see you," Amy said earnestly. "We're friends of Kat, your niece, and we think she may be in trouble."

"Kat, in trouble?" Lizzie sounded concerned. "Come in and sit down." She led them into a living room with huge picture windows overlooking the patchwork of the city below. Rather than a red brick sprawl, most of it was green: trees, parks and gardens, with hills beyond. Lizzie's furniture looked old and battered, but homely. Bright crocheted throws covered the seats; prints of foreign seaside towns lined the walls.

Tea was already in the be-cosied pot. Lizzie poured the amber liquid into mismatched mugs, adding milk straight from a bottle. "Kat isn't exactly my niece," she said. "But I look on her like a daughter. What's wrong?"

"We don't know," Ross said. "She vanished four days ago."

Amy nodded. The alleged theft and sham marriages were probably the cause of the disappearance. She couldn't tell Lizzie in front of Ross, though, or even mention the knifeman.

102

"What are the police doing?" Lizzie asked.

"Not much," Amy admitted. "They told me they'd look into it."

"You want to find her then?" Lizzie asked.

"Of course," Ross said. "I've got air tickets to Thailand for both of us." He was clearly playing for sympathy.

"The penny's dropped," Lizzie said. "You're her boyfriend. I thought the two of you…" she pointed to Amy and Ross.

"I'm just a friend," Amy said. She was rapidly tiring of the inference, implicit in the assumptions of everyone they met, that Ross was attractive to women. A handsome face and bank balance simply couldn't compensate for his repulsive personality. She marvelled at his ability to keep the latter hidden when it suited him. "Listen, do you have any idea where she is? You said you weren't her aunt, but she must have family in the area?"

"No and no," Lizzie replied. "Erik's the only family she has in this country, if he's still here, of course. Goodness knows where he might be. I doubt I'd even recognise him."

"Erik?" Amy asked.

"Her brother," Lizzie replied. "I can see from your blank faces, you really don't know much about Kat do you?"

"I'm sure you can put that right," Ross murmured.

Lizzie cackled. "Your pillow talk can't be up to much, young man. All right, I'll tell you what I can. Kat and Erik aren't from Birmingham at all. They're not even English, although they've got English passports now. Marty saw to it."

"Marty?" Ross asked.

"I'll come to that. Don't worry; he's not competition for you. Kat's Russian. Her father sent the two children to boarding school in England. She speaks very properly, doesn't she? Not like me!" Lizzie chuckled throatily. "They needed a local guardian, which is where Marty Bridges came in. He did a lot of business with their father – importing vodka. Everything was grand. Then the father fell out with his government."

"What happened?" Amy wanted to know.

"They killed him. Not at first. He was in prison for a bit. They wanted him to sign some papers, but he refused. The children were stranded here." She frowned. "The boy, Erik, managed all right. He was grown up by then, at university. Kat was at her lovely school, and they made her leave. No money for the fees, you see." She gulped the remaining tea from her mug, and poured herself another. Despite adding a generous slug of milk, it remained dark as her teak dining chairs. Lizzie drank it regardless. "You with me so far?"

Amy nodded.

"Good. I know I've been round the Wrekin. Kat was sixteen, with nowhere to go. I felt sorry for her, so I took her in here. My husband had just died and I was glad of the company. She worked as a cleaner and in a shop to earn her keep, then she trained as a croupier. Like a flash, she was off to London." She sniffed. "I wish she'd stayed here. I could tell from her letters it was a dangerous place. Not all of her friends were very nice. Present company excepted, I should say."

"What friends?" Ross asked.

"There was a fellow called Jeb who used to help her out with money." Lizzie glanced at Ross. His face was distinctly unamused.

"She was teaching Jeb maths," Amy lied, to her own amazement. She had to divert Ross' attention to a different topic. "How did you meet Kat?" she asked Lizzie.

"I was Marty's housekeeper," Lizzie said. "Not that I'd have anything to do with him now. Dirty old man."

"What do you mean?" Ross' voice was stern.

"Not in that way," Lizzie said. "He remarried with indecent haste after his first wife died, that's all. His new one's a common, stuck-up bitch, if you'll pardon my French. It wasn't right, and I told him."

"Would he know where Kat is?" Ross asked.

Lizzie shrugged. "You could ask him. He might help, but I don't suppose he will if he can't see anything in it for him. He's hard as

104

nails." She added, "He lives on Wellington Road. I don't know where his office is – I've never been there."

"Thank you," Ross said smarmily. "You really have been tremendously helpful."

"You're welcome," Lizzie preened. "Come round any time if you want to know anything else. I hope you have a nice holiday with her. Send me a postcard."

She waved cheerily as they exited into the lift lobby.

"Marty Bridges is our next port of call," Ross said, with the optimistic tone of a man who felt he was making progress. "We should grab lunch first. There were a couple of promising pubs near Treasures. Let's eat there."

Chapter 19 Jeb

Jeb scooped up a spoonful of chilli. "It's vegetarian," he complained.

"That's what the little 'v' on the menu means," Shaun said.

If anyone else had made such a derisive remark, Jeb would have thumped them. He was touchy on the matter of his literacy. The schools he had attended were not the best, he felt, although he conceded that he could have turned up for lessons more often. He contented himself with a surly glare. "Doesn't taste bad, though," he said.

"It's a yuppie pub," Shaun said. "You can tell from the beer prices. If you thought it was cheaper up north, think again."

Driven outside by their nicotine habits, they were sitting on benches in the beer garden of a pub a few doors away from Treasures. The weather in Birmingham was sultry, although an occasional raindrop and hint of a breeze cut through the sticky air. A group of young men in business-casual clothes and black-rimmed spectacles sat nearby, chatting and working on laptops.

"Those would be worth nicking," Jeb observed. He was still racking his brains for a way to raise twenty thousand pounds. His life depended on it. Shaun hadn't put the squeeze on him yet, but only because his boss believed Kat was the culprit. That delusion would vanish as soon as Shaun found her. It was essential, then, that Shaun didn't find Kat, or at least didn't find her alive.

Of course, with Kat dead, Shaun would still look to Jeb to make good the stolen money. None remained. Once he'd given cash to Kat and Ahmed, and paid for cocaine he'd been given to sell and recklessly consumed himself, there had been very little left. That was gone too, thanks to bad decisions at the racetrack and gaming tables.

Jeb squirmed, fearing the mysterious Lizzie and the role she might play in reuniting Kat with Shaun. If only he could somehow see her alone and neutralise the threat she posed to him. He finished his chilli with a nervous belch, and lit a cigarette.

Shaun was squinting at the laptops. "You're right; they're MacBooks," he said. "See the Apple symbols? Three hundred quid each, no questions asked." He drained his pint. "Another lager, Jeb? That'll be your last. I want you to drive back later."

Jeb wiped sweat from his brow. "So I've got to watch like a thirsty ferret while you drink all afternoon. Are you sure you don't have the old bag's address?"

Shaun handed him the letter. "Read it yourself," he said cruelly. He fingered his chin. "Actually, Jeb, you're on to something. That fit blonde said she was called Lizzie Clements. I bet I can find her online." He glanced at the young workers with their laptops.

"How do you do that?" Jeb knew the keystrokes required to access online video games and porn. Other than that, computers were a mystery to him.

"The boys showed me." Shaun took his BlackBerry from his pocket.

"I'll get the drinks in," Jeb said hastily.

Shaun was grinning when he returned. "Sorted!" the older man said. He waved the BlackBerry at Jeb. "You've got one of these too. Look, just type in her postcode and it'll give you directions."

Shaun demonstrated the function, causing his own phone to tell him in a schoolmarm's voice: "Turn right. Walk one hundred yards."

"See?" Shaun laughed.

"Well, save the beer for me, boss," Jeb said, "I'll go there right now. You watch the footie on that screen inside."

Shaun didn't argue. Whistling with relief, Jeb left the pub, almost kicking small children out of the way as he rushed along the suburban high street. His BlackBerry directed him down a side road and an alleyway. Jeb approached it with trepidation. Strangers using such lanes near his home were likely to be relieved of their valuables, or at least meet sullen teenagers succumbing to addictions away from the watchful glances of their parents. His journey passed without incident, however, and within minutes he was laboriously punching Lizzie Clements' number into the tower block's intercom.

"I'm a friend of Kat's," he said.

"Another one!" she exclaimed, giving him cause for alarm. Jeb sniffed a precautionary pinch of cocaine for courage, first scanning the lift lobby for CCTV cameras. Much to his relief, he found none.

Lizzie looked old enough to be his grandmother, although that didn't predispose Jeb to be either gentle or respectful towards her. He was sentimentally affectionate to his own mother and grandmother, without caring a jot for anyone else's. His first action on stepping across her threshold was to remove a flick-knife from his sock.

Her eyes almost popped out of their wrinkled sockets with shock. Lizzie shrank away from him, uttering a piercing shriek.

"Don't do that," he shouted, punching her cheek. There was a sickening crack. He cursed, hoping she could still talk. "Where's Kat?" he screamed at her.

"I don't know."

Jeb hadn't considered that possibility. Shaun had been so sure they would find Kat with Lizzie. Only now did Jeb recall that Kat had never mentioned this aunt at all, had in fact told him nothing about herself other than saying her parents were dead. That was a gold star in his book; the fewer people who knew or cared about his girls, the better. It was even more of a bonus at this stage, when he wanted Kat dead and would do whatever it took to achieve it.

He raised a fist to Lizzie. "You're lying," he said.

"What's all this about? What do you want," she whimpered, beginning to cry.

"Stop that," Jeb growled. "Tell me where she is." He slapped her left ear, not using his full weight this time, but enough to sting.

"If I knew, I'd tell you," Lizzie sobbed.

He realised the futility of his questions then, and changed tack. "Who was here earlier?" he yelled. "Who?"

"Her boyfriend."

That made no sense to Jeb. Kat had never mentioned a relationship. He was sure he would have been aware had she taken a lover. "You're lying again." He was furious. What right did she have to waste his time? He slapped her face.

The old woman tripped backwards, hitting her crown on the coffee table. Jeb heard a cracking sound once more. Blood seeped from her skull.

Wild-eyed, Jeb checked for a pulse. He had some experience of this, living among addicts who were prone to overdose on substances of uncertain purity. Fumbling at Lizzie's wrist, he felt no evidence of a heartbeat. Too bad, he thought. As it happened, she'd known so little that there was no need to kill her. This way, though, she wouldn't be telling anyone about their little chat.

Just as he rose to leave, the corner of his eye twitched. Something was moving to his left. Jeb swivelled round. A thin black cat, its fur patchy and its gait creaky, was creeping towards the door. "Don't spy on me," Jeb said coldly. He kicked the animal out of his way. In his haste, he overlooked the flick-knife lying on the floor.

Chapter 20 Amy

The pubs Ross had spotted were a large roadhouse advertising lunches for five pounds, and a more upmarket establishment facing it across the high street. As Amy expected, he insisted on lunch at the latter. They ordered food at the bar.

"A large dry white wine," Ross said, "and a pint of Doom Bar."

She looked askance at him. "Are you feeling all right, Ross?"

He didn't twig at first. "Of course," he said eventually. "The beer. I am on holiday, you know."

There was a conservatory at the rear of the pub, and a garden beyond that. Amy suggested they sat outside in the sunshine. Ross appeared ready to squabble, then noticed a young woman in the pub breastfeeding her baby. He glowed bright red, agreeing that a sunny spot was an excellent idea.

The first table outside was occupied by hipsters comparing the latest Apple gadgets with each other. As she walked past them, Amy caught sight of the knifeman.

At first, she wasn't sure it was really him. He was sitting alone on a wooden bench, a near-empty pint in his hand and another on the table in front of him. His eyes were fixed on the super-sized TV screen inside the conservatory.

"Let's sit over there, Amy." Ross gestured to the nearest free table.

At those words, the knifeman looked straight at her. His relaxed demeanour was replaced by the wary, almost haunted expression she remembered from his visit. She had no remaining doubts about his identity.

He could have none about hers either, for he was rising to his feet. Amy thrust her wine glass on the table occupied by the surprised hipsters. She pulled at Ross' free hand. "Ross, run! Leave your drink. We have to get out of here."

Her colleague's lips began to move. With a grimace of exasperation, she said, "Just for once, don't argue, Ross. Just run, as fast as you can."

To his credit, he did as he was told, and commendably quickly. His untouched pint was left on the nearest table; he sprinted back into the pub and out through the main door onto the high street. Amy wasn't as fit or fast, but, holding his hand, she was dragged along at the same speed by his momentum.

She heard the knifeman shout. He must be following. Desperately, she prayed for a cab to materialise on the busy road outside.

"There's a taxi," Ross cried, the sweetest words he'd ever said to her. As he flagged it down, she saw the pub door opening again. Ross virtually shoved her into the vehicle, following swiftly and slamming its door in the face of their pursuer.

"Is he with you?" the driver asked, jerking a thumb at the knifeman.

"No." Amy was aware she sounded hysterical. Hearing the click of the cab doors locking, she breathed a sigh of relief.

"Where do you want to go?"

"I don't know," she said. She was still panicking, panting breathlessly. "Anywhere."

"The Malmaison Hotel," Ross interjected. "Do it in five minutes and I'll double your money." He lowered his voice to a whisper. "For crying out loud, Amy," he hissed, "what's going on?"

"That was someone I didn't want to meet, that's all," she said, staring out of the window as suburbia flashed past. The cabbie was making a valiant effort to win his bonus. "It's just a coincidence."

Ross looked daggers at her, but he was silent for the rest of their short journey.

Chapter 21 Jeb

Jeb had left Shaun enjoying a quiet pint. He imagined his boss would be in a mellow mood on his return, but not a bit of it.

"Where have you been?" Shaun asked, his voice low but withering.

Jeb looked around. The iPad users were still chattering at the next table, which doubtless explained why Shaun's explosion was controlled. "I found the aunt," he whispered.

"And?" Shaun was evidently hoping for more. "What about Kat?"

"She wasn't there," Jeb admitted. "Her aunt hadn't seen her."

Shaun reddened. "Did you search the aunt's flat and put the frighteners on her?"

"Turned the place over," Jeb lied. "Nothing. To cap it all, the old biddy went and died on me."

"How?" Shaun was even less amused.

"Heart attack," Jeb said smoothly. "On my mother's life, I only hit her once."

Shaun put his head in his hands. "Let's get out of this city," he muttered. "It'll be too hot for us once the body's found." He drained his pint in one. "You're driving, Jeb."

The Merc was round the corner where Shaun had left it, intact as far as Jeb could tell. Shaun said little until they were on the M6.

"Kat must be in that misbegotten city," he said to Jeb, "because I saw her flatmate in the pub."

"Amy?" Jeb asked. He had seen, and ignored, Amy several times when visiting Kat to take her drinking in Charlotte Street. She was flat-chested, straight-laced, and simply of no concern to him. "A coincidence, boss. She's from round here." He knew none of his words were true.

Shaun must have suspected it, for he said sharply, "Amy doesn't have a Birmingham accent."

"Nor does Kat," Jeb extemporised.

112

That seemed to satisfy Shaun, at least for a few minutes. He relapsed into gloomy silence. As the car passed another motorway junction, he said, "I knew I was missing something. Snow Mountain."

"Oh, the vodka?" Jeb said. "Kat's dad used to sell it."

He cursed himself for saying it. Until then, he thought he'd deflected his boss from Kat's trail, but Shaun's reaction was immediate. "That's it. Turn the car around. We're going to see that Bridges fellow."

"Are you sure?" Jeb asked. "I thought you had to get back to take some deliveries."

"We've got time to see Bridges first," Shaun said, grabbing the satnav. "The office is in the city centre," he mused. "He must have more money than sense."

Jeb did a U-turn at the next junction, his heart heavy as they neared the sleek glass offices of downtown Birmingham. He had realised to his horror that his flick-knife was missing.

Bridges' premises were just outside the central area, in fact, in a road of factories and warehouses not unlike the trading estate where Shaun's speakeasy was located. The car park next to it was full. Jeb parked on double yellow lines, paying no heed to Shaun's frown. It wasn't as if he had a choice.

Shaun jumped out of the car, striding towards the dismal grey door that appeared to be the only entrance to the property. There was a buzzer next to it. Shaun pressed it eagerly, waiting several moments before a disembodied female voice said, "Yes?"

"I want to see Marty Bridges," Shaun said. "I'm a customer."

"Well, he's not here." The woman sounded bored.

"Where is he?"

"Out. Do you have an appointment?"

Jeb could see Shaun was about to protest. He motioned to the CCTV cameras in the building's eaves. Two were trained on the door.

Shaun nodded, scowling. "When will he be back?"

"Come here tomorrow," she said.

113

Chapter 22 Ross

A morning of Amy's company was as much as he could take, Ross decided. At the Malmaison, he told her he wanted to spend the afternoon and evening alone. He would order from room service, and he suggested she did the same.

Their flight from the pub had unnerved him. It not only demonstrated how annoying Amy was – after all, they'd travelled a hundred miles and she could still encounter someone who disliked her – but it revealed a startling layer of dishonesty. She knew more about Kat's disappearance than she'd told him. How were they supposed to work together when she was withholding information from him? Ross sat in his room, sipping a beer at last. Of course, Amy might argue that he didn't need to know everything; that her secrets were of no consequence in their search. Ross' lips pursed. He would rather be the judge of that.

Lizzie, too, almost certainly knew more than she had divulged. At least he had Erik and Marty's names, and half of Marty's address. Ross began to search online. Erik, he assumed, would have the same surname as Kat: White. If what Lizzie said was true, it almost certainly wasn't the name on his birth certificate. With no other information about Erik, Ross drew a blank. He was more successful with Martyn Bridges, obtaining the number of the house in Wellington Road, and of commercial premises in Florence Street.

Ross saw that Florence Street was a short stroll from his hotel, and decided to walk there at once. Just to be sure of seeing Bridges, he phoned ahead for an appointment. He was told Bridges was away on business that day but would be available in the morning. His staff would not supply personal contact details.

Ross paid a modest fee to a website that claimed to hold twenty million UK telephone numbers. He was given one for Wellington Road, but no one answered it when he called. Rather vexed, Ross spent an hour in the hotel gym before a few ruthless hands of online poker saw his bank balance increase even further. He paced his hotel room restlessly, bored. While he might have taken a more congenial travelling companion to dinner, he decided to leave Amy to her own devices and explore Birmingham by himself. Behind the hotel, there were several bars overlooking a canal lined with brightly painted houseboats. He sat outside with a beer, appreciating the short skirts of the young women passing by, if not their local accents. Finally, he took the lift to the top of the Cube, a squarish skyscraper mosaicked like a randomly-completed jigsaw. Here, he enjoyed a rare steak and a panoramic view of the city. Away from his daily routine, it felt like his holiday was beginning.

After the intensity of his day, Ross wanted an early night. Another beer sent him soundly to sleep in his hotel bed. The rest stood him in good stead, as he was surprised to be woken at six by the West Midlands Police.

They knocked on his door just as he was starting to rub sleep from his eyes. He was an early riser from habit; he liked to visit the gym before breakfast. "Police. Open up."

Somewhat alarmed, Ross did as requested. The two men outside were uniformed, so although he asked them for identification, he didn't spend much time examining it before letting them into the room. "I'm Ross Pritchard," he said smoothly, extending a hand to each of them in turn. Neither responded with a handshake. Taken aback, Ross asked, "To what do I owe the pleasure?"

"I'm arresting you on suspicion of the attempted murder of Elizabeth Clements," the younger of the two, identified as Darren Donnelly, said. "You do not have to say anything. But, it may harm your defence if you do not mention when questioned something which you later rely on in court. Anything you do say may be given in evidence."

"This is a joke, isn't it?" Ross asked. Although it would be an elaborate prank, and he struggled to imagine who'd arranged it, he couldn't believe the men were serious.

"Not at all," Donnelly said. He and his colleague remained poker-faced. "Did you take a taxi from Harborne High Street yesterday?"

"Yes." Ross had no idea why that might be of interest, and was about to say so.

"And you also saw Elizabeth Clements?"

"You mean Lizzie? Someone's tried to murder her?" Ross was dumbfounded.

"Did you see her?" Donnelly persisted.

"Yes," Ross admitted.

"Thank you, Mr Pritchard. We're taking you to the police station, where we will be asking you to give a full account of your movements yesterday."

"In that case," Ross said, still shocked, and sensing he might spend several hours in their company, "you will let me get dressed first, and I'll also need to ask the hotel to extend my stay." The cost was hardly an issue for a man of his means, especially as his tax-free poker winnings yesterday had been substantial.

As they left his room, he saw Amy, similarly accompanied. He'd made an effort to look professional in a suit, shirt and tie, even wearing spectacles he only really needed for screen work. Amy, by contrast, appeared tired and drained, hair unkempt and skin free of make-up. Ross had little sympathy for her. She ought to learn to wake earlier, especially if she was dragging him into a criminal investigation. "Boo," he said.

Amy glared at him. Her eyes were red and moist.

"I suppose you know what this is all about?" he asked her.

"No." Amy's voice was subdued, her expression puzzled.

The bewilderment might be an act. He couldn't trust her. Nevertheless, he hissed at Amy, "Tell them nothing. I'm getting both of us a good lawyer. It's no comment until then. Understand?" He remembered an old school friend, a criminal lawyer, telling him this was the best strategy and one used by all his long-standing clients. Saying nothing, they couldn't either implicate themselves or find their words misconstrued before he arrived on the scene.

Donnelly scowled at Amy, the WPCs with her, and finally at Ross. "Come along, Mr Pritchard. We haven't got all day."

"Have you got that?" Ross yelled at Amy.

"Yes," she nodded.

He was allowed to speak briefly to the single member of staff on the hotel reception desk, a young woman whose professional polish was unaffected by the presence of police. Having extended their stay for two nights, he and Amy were taken away in separate cars. He glimpsed hers arriving as he was led into the police station, a gracious old red brick building. Still astonished by the turn of events, he wondered what awaited him behind its pretty exterior.

Chapter 23 Amy

Her tears had dried but the shock of her arrest remained. While her mind was in turmoil, Amy nevertheless realised Ross was right. She said nothing as the police car sped past the glittering offices of central Birmingham in the early morning quiet. It had rained overnight and the streets were still shiny, the air fresh and cool. Arriving at the Steelhouse Lane police station, she shivered in her thin summer dress.

"It's warmer inside," said one of the WPCs with her, and indeed it was, as the windows were closed and barred. Amy was taken to an interview room, simply furnished with plastic chairs and a laminate table.

"You do appreciate," Amy said haltingly, "I won't be making any statement until my solicitor arrives?"

"When will he be here?"

"I don't know. Ross is arranging it."

"Your boyfriend?"

Amy shook her head, weary of explaining once again that Ross wasn't her boyfriend.

The two WPCs exchanged glances. "You can see the duty solicitor if you like."

"No thank you." Although there didn't seem to be any harm in the suggestion, she had given Ross her word. She would wait, as he'd asked her to.

"We're going to have to leave you in a cell, then."

The cell was as Amy might have expected from a TV drama: a box-like room, painted white, with a barred window. The only seating was a bed with a thin mattress. Her handbag was taken from her, and with no phone, she had little idea of the time. After what seemed hours, she was given a mug of tea and two slices of buttered white toast. She thought longingly of the lavish breakfast on the London train, and the undoubtedly even larger spread on offer at the Malmaison.

Fortunately, her solicitor arrived not long afterwards. The cell door was unlocked and she was asked to accompany the same WPCs to the interview room. The lawyer held out her hand.

Although barely older than Amy, tall and ebony-skinned with close-cropped hair, she had a polish that screamed of money. Her manicured nails were flawless, her navy linen dress was perfectly pressed and her shoes were Louboutins. Amy was sure of it; they were identical to a pair Kat owned.

"Lulu Lawson," she said, dark eyes scrutinising Amy. Her patrician voice spoke of money just as much as her appearance. "I work for Ted Edwards, who went to school with your boyfriend and who's with him right now."

"He's not my boyfriend," Amy protested, noting sceptical grins from the two WPCs. Lulu should already be aware of that, surely? Amy wasn't inspired with confidence in the lawyer.

"Sorry," Lulu apologised. She turned to the police officers. "I'd like some time alone with my client, especially as you can see we don't know each other very well."

They acceded without a murmur. It was obviously normal procedure for them.

"Do forgive me," Lulu said. "It took us three hours to get here. Quite a trek from London."

"Isn't it?" Amy agreed. "Ross and I travelled up yesterday."

Lulu stared at her. "You came here from London, and within twenty four hours you're facing an attempted murder charge. Would you mind talking me through everything? First of all, why did you go to Birmingham?"

"We were looking for my flatmate."

"Tell me about her," Lulu said, "and why you travelled a hundred miles to look for her. By the way, our conversation is totally confidential. The police don't need to know about it. Ross told Ted you were keeping secrets. Well, you shouldn't hold anything back

119

from me. Whatever happens, I'll say nothing without your consent. Is that OK?"

Amy nodded. "Kat's my flatmate," she said, "and a few weeks ago, she married an illegal immigrant called Ahmed Khan. She stole my identity to do it."

"Have you told the police?" Lulu said.

"Yes, when Kat disappeared five days ago, I ended up telling them. They thought I'd really married Ahmed Khan."

"I don't mean to worry you," Lulu said, "but if you had married him, you would be Mrs Khan in the eyes of the law. Although it's an immigration offence, it's still a marriage."

"Is Kat actually married to him then?"

Lulu touched her arm. "That's her problem. Let's concentrate on you. When Kat vanished, why did you go looking for her? Why not just let the police do it?"

"I didn't think the police believed me," Amy said. "Also, I thought she was in danger. There were strange visitors. One man had a key to the flat. I found him searching through Kat's room. He took a couple of potted plants."

"Really?" Lulu's eyes widened.

Despite her predicament, Amy laughed. Lulu might as well have had a thought bubble rising from her head. "Not cannabis," she said. "I don't know what they were. He claimed they were his. He was looking for something else that belonged to him, but he didn't find it."

"How bizarre," Lulu said. "You said a couple of visitors. Who was the other one?"

"Neither exactly introduced themselves," Amy said. "The second man was scary." She described her encounter with the knifeman.

"Do the police know about these men?" Lulu's face was grim.

"No."

"I think that knowledge would help them."

"Even Ross doesn't know."

120

"That's between you and him," Lulu said. "Anyway, please put me in the picture. How does Ross fit into this?"

As Lulu listened attentively, Amy told her everything: how Ross, her colleague, was infatuated with Kat and they'd tracked down Lizzie. Of course, the knifeman knew about Lizzie too. "It was a shock to see him in a pub garden in Birmingham," Amy said, "but I should have seen it coming!"

"You couldn't anticipate that," Lulu reassured her. "On the other hand, the police reaction is everything I'd expect. Imagine you're in their shoes. Lizzie Clements is discovered close to death. They know you've visited her. As soon as they release your description, a cab driver comes forward to say you took a taxi to the city centre in a hurry. They have no knowledge of the knifeman. What are they going to think?"

She didn't have to say more. "I see what you mean," Amy said.

"Exactly," Lulu said. "It will help you if you tell them what you've told me. It will help Kat as well. Those men are dangerous. They're not planning to see her for a cup of tea, are they?"

Amy shivered, recalling the knifeman's twitching mouth, the way he'd stroked his blade. She nodded.

"Okay," Lulu said. "I suggest we prepare a statement together, hand it over and ask them to release you."

"Will they?"

"They might. I suspect they've taken statements from Linda Sweetman and the cab driver. That'll suggest you, or someone who looks like you, was in Harborne. You'll not only confirm that, avoiding the need for an identity parade, but you'll volunteer a great deal more to them. It will help your case. You'd hardly admit to visiting Lizzie Clements if you really tried to murder her, would you?"

"I guess not."

"Well then," Lulu removed a thin silver laptop from her soft leather handbag, "Let's get working on that statement."

It was typed within an hour. "Take a look and see if you agree," Lulu said. "Also, if there's anything you haven't mentioned that strikes you as odd, let me know."

"There is one thing," Amy said. "It isn't so much that Kat had a visitor, but that she didn't. I haven't seen Jeb for at least a week, and that's unusual." She realised now that it had niggled her when Linda Sweetman mentioned two men. She couldn't imagine the plantsman and knifeman working in tandem. The knifeman and Jeb, with their Cockney accents and cold eyes, were a different matter entirely.

"Who's Jeb – her boyfriend?"

"No, he's never stayed over. He just takes Kat out for drinks, cocktails in a bar like Sykes on Charlotte Street." Amy wished she could afford a night out in the pulsing heart of Fitzrovia. Of course, Kat never bought her own drinks. That was part of Jeb's attraction. There was his bad boy image too, and here, Amy struggled to find the right words. "I have no proof that Jeb's a gangster, but Kat suggested he was. I think he was just a bit of rough for her, a Cockney boy from Canning Town." He took cocaine and probably sold it as well, or how could someone of his background afford a sporty BMW? Kat had intimated once that Jeb could hardly read. She didn't care, though. A croupier was hardly in a position to be an intellectual snob. Jeb made her laugh, she said.

"You described the other two men," Lulu said. "Let me look at my notes. The first was exceptionally tall and thin, with a long nose, green eyes, spiky black hair thinning at the crown. He was solemn and rarely smiled, and he was possibly in his late twenties. The second: average height, neat black hair turning to grey, blue eyes, pale skin, slim but the start of a paunch and jowls. He was your father's age or thereabouts, so late forties. Could you give a description of Jeb as well?"

"Jeb's probably the tallest of the three, and he's broad as well. Not fat, but well-muscled. His hair is like yours."

"He's black?"

"Mixed race," Amy said. "His skin's light brown."

"Anything else?"

"He's about thirty. He wears a nose ring and a single earring."

"Thank you," Lulu smiled. "Let's see what the police make of that."

To Amy's relief, Lulu was right. As soon as her statement had been printed and signed, she was free to leave.

"I rather think Ross will be allowed to go too," Lulu said. "Let's have a coffee while we wait for Ted to ring." She checked her smartphone. "There's a place round the corner."

It was two hours before Ross and Ted joined them. Ted, a stocky, sandy-haired fellow as ugly as Ross was handsome, immediately congratulated Amy.

"I have to hand it to you," he said. "You gave them the man's name and description."

"Who do you mean?" Amy asked, bemused. She didn't know the mysterious visitors' names.

"Jebediah Bryant," Ted said. "That's who the police want now. If I'm not much mistaken, we'll find they've issued an appeal for information on his whereabouts."

"Jeb?" Amy said.

"The very same. Your evidence was, as it happens, corroborated by the police forensics team who found his fingerprint on a knife left at the scene."

"What happened to Lizzie?" Amy asked. "No one told me. I hope she's okay."

"As okay as anyone can be when they've been seriously duffed up," Ted said. "From what I can make out, he just gave her the rough stuff. Used his fists on her. Took it out on the cat as well. God knows why he left a knife. He didn't cut her with it."

"To threaten her," Amy murmured, shuddering.

"Look, do you think we could buy some lunch?" Ross said peevishly.

"Amy and I have already eaten," Lulu said. "I recommend the paninis. The coffee's good too."

"I could use a beer," Ted said. "I see a few bottles over there. Are you up for it, Ross? Then we'll have a de-brief."

"Get a large glass of white wine for Amy too, will you?" Ross said. For the first time, he smiled at her.

"I honestly don't think the boys in blue will bother you again," Ted said when the food and drinks had arrived. "They've released you without charge. Now they'll focus on finding Jebediah and building a case against him."

"We don't know what the victim will say," Lulu cautioned.

"True," Ted agreed. "Jebediah obviously meant to finish her off. She's in a coma, I believe, but expected to recover. That'll be a shock for him. But whatever the old biddy tells them, it lets our clients off the hook, doesn't it?"

"We must find Kat," Ross said. "If Jebediah's after her, he won't make the same mistake twice." A shadow crossed his face and he stared at Amy. "You say he isn't Kat's boyfriend, but what is he to her? Why do you think he's doing this?"

"I don't know," Amy said, blurting out, "I just can't make sense of it."

Lulu touched her arm again. "The police will."

"What exactly has been going on?" Ross said. He looked confused and miserable.

Amy took a deep breath. How could she ever have imagined she could hide the truth from him? Now the police were involved, everyone's secrets would be revealed. "There are other people looking for Kat," she began.

She told him about the visitors to the flat, Jeb's frequent presence and the sham marriages. "This is just a guess," she said, "but I think Jeb might have played a part in the marriages. Maybe he introduced the happy couples. The last groom was a chef from Bangladesh. Kat

124

would never normally meet someone like that. The only foreigners she knows are the rich gamblers who play at Diamonds."

"Could they be involved in the wedding scam?" Lulu asked.

"Unlikely," Ted interrupted. "The UK wants to attract the wealthy, not throw them out. Are you saying, Amy, that Jebediah is a shady character who would know the other sort of foreigner?"

"Exactly," Amy agreed.

"I bet Jebediah forced Kat into those marriages," Ross said hotly. "Why else would she make such a massive error of judgement?"

Because she saw pound signs in front of her eyes, Amy was tempted to say. Instead, she asked for another glass of wine.

"Well, old boy," Ted said, "it's been good to catch up with you. Lulu and I are back to London now. There's a court case in the morning. No peace for the wicked."

"You can call us if you need us, though," Lulu said.

Ross ordered more drinks at the counter. "That wasn't how I planned to spend my day," he admitted ruefully. "I wish I'd known more about this. I had no idea Kat was in such dreadful danger, or what you'd been through, for that matter."

"I can understand why she doesn't want to be found," Amy said.

"Yes," he said. "Well, we won't find her today. Let's head back to the Malmaison. I fancy playing more poker. Ted's fees don't come cheap." He smiled at her for the second time. "We should have dinner together later, then we can work out what to do next. Marty Bridges is our next line of enquiry, I think."

"Be careful, Ross," Amy said. Her irritation towards him was diminishing. At last she felt they were a team, and suddenly, his welfare was a concern. "We don't know what Marty looks like. He could be the man we saw in Harborne – the man who held a knife to my throat."

"I'm not convinced," Ross said. "He's a businessman in Birmingham. Why would he be skulking in shadows in a London car park? I'll google him. I'm sure I can find an image."

Chapter 24 Shaun

"I could have done this by myself," Jeb grumbled.

Shaun winced at the thought, although his frustration was mounting. He'd wasted a full day thanks to Marty Bridges, and now they'd been sitting for twenty minutes on uncomfortable plastic chairs in Bridges' reception lobby.

It was even blander and more boring than AKD's. Unlike AKD, it was unmanned, with no decorative receptionist to catch Shaun's eye. Jeb appeared restless, probably coming down from yesterday's amphetamines. Despite the lobby sign urging them not to smoke, the younger man was puffing on a cigarette. He continued when the shabby white office door opened and a short, balding fellow emerged.

Shaun knew the type well. Bridges would be stupid and opinionated. He would have inherited his business from his father, not quite managed to run it into the ground, and be full of his own importance.

Bridges first words to them didn't disappoint. "There's no smoking on my premises, thank you."

"Jeb, go outside," Shaun said. Jeb complied, glaring at both of them.

"You phoned before," Bridges said. "I haven't changed my mind, I'm afraid. I can't spare any Snow Mountain for you. I've got a range of flavoured vodkas that's popular in the clubs, though. Why not taste a few of those while you're here?"

"Do you know who I am?" Shaun asked, allowing an edge of menace to creep into his voice.

Bridges actually laughed. "Yes," he said, "you own a seedy dive in the backstreets of London. That's exactly the sort of place where I don't want Snow Mountain on display. It's a premium product for a reason."

"You need to show more respect." Jeb, returning to the lobby, towered over Bridges.

Shaun looked meaningfully at the CCTV camera, a silent watchdog in a corner of the room. They had to be careful. If Bridges allowed them into his office, Jeb could be more persuasive.

"It's not a problem," he said. "Yes, I would like a tasting, please."

"Come on through." Bridges gestured to the door. A corridor stretched behind it. Bridges took them to a heavy oak door with the name 'Mr Bridges' etched onto a brass nameplate. Inside, his office was wood-panelled and crammed with imposing furniture, as Shaun had expected it would be. "Sit down." Bridges pointed to black leather chairs clustered around a polished table.

Shaun's bones were aching from nearly half an hour in a moulded plastic seat. He sank gratefully into a padded chair. He noticed Jeb still appeared on edge.

"You see?" Bridges waved a hand at his desk, adorned with six brightly coloured bottles. "I've got a plain one, lemon, chocolate, chilli – that's popular with the lads – vanilla and peach. You're not driving are you, gentlemen?"

"I am," Shaun said. He had no intention of sampling the disgusting, sticky drinks. Jeb was welcome to do so; it might calm him down.

"I'll have a cup of tea made for you." Bridges turned his back to them. "Let me get some glasses from the cupboard first."

"Now," Shaun ordered. Jeb retrieved his knife from his sock.

Bridges nearly dropped his shot glasses when he saw it. "Why are you waving that around?" he demanded.

"For fun," Jeb grinned, advancing on his prey.

"Not so fast, Jeb," Shaun said sharply, stepping between them to form a barrier. "Remember, we're here to get information, that's all."

"And I thought you just wanted a drink," Bridges said, flashing a smile that didn't meet his eyes.

"I'll have vodka too," Shaun said. "Twenty four bottles of Snow Mountain."

"Then I'd better get the keys to the warehouse," Bridges said, sidling around to his rather grand office desk and opening a drawer.

Chapter 25 Amy

Relieved to be out in the fresh air, Amy walked back to the hotel with Ross. Although it was only a short distance, perhaps a mile, she felt tired. Fatigue was flooding into her as her tension released and the wine took effect. "I'm going to crash out as soon as we're back."

"Why don't you go to the hotel spa?" Ross suggested unexpectedly. "Ladies seem to like them."

"I can't afford it."

"Don't worry about that," Ross said magnanimously. "Charge it to your room. I'll pick up the tab."

Amy didn't need telling twice. An aromatherapy massage was just what she needed after the rigours of the day. She was happy and relaxed when she joined Ross for dinner in the hotel restaurant.

"Shall we start with a bottle of white wine?" Ross asked.

She was seeing a different side to him now. The old Ross would have told her what wine they were having, if indeed he'd ordered any.

"I found Marty's profile on LinkedIn," Ross said, "complete with photo. I can assure you categorically that he is not the man we saw in that pub. Having established that, I phoned him to say I had a business proposition for him."

"Do you?" Amy could barely disguise her disbelief.

"Of course not," Ross said. "He agreed to a meeting, though. We'll see him tomorrow at ten."

"We still don't know much about him," Amy said, "except that Lizzie said he was hard as nails." She doubted Marty would be well-disposed towards them.

"Don't worry," Ross said. "I'm used to dealing with difficult people. I have to handle Cari every day for starters."

"She's your boss, isn't she; the short woman with bright red hair? I don't know what you're complaining about. You've met Parveen."

"Parveen is the nursery slopes," Ross said gloomily. "Cari is a grade A bitch. In medieval times, redheads were burned as witches. I wish we could still do it today."

"Tactful as usual, Ross," Amy said, pointing to her own auburn locks.

Ross refused to let her crush his ego. "Can't you take a joke? Relax, Amy. We've just escaped an attempted murder charge and we should celebrate. Forget the white wine. Let's order champagne."

He seemed almost charming after that, although the champagne undoubtedly helped. Amy found herself telling Ross her life story.

"I really thought a degree in marketing would be the passport to my dream job," she said, "but churning out policy literature for Parveen definitely isn't it."

"What's your degree?" Ross asked, topping up her glass.

"A 2:2 in marketing from the University of the West of England," Amy said.

"There's your answer," Ross said. "You need a first for the best jobs, like the actuarial stream at Veritable."

Amy chose her words carefully. Actuarial work featured at the foot of her wish list, along with sewage disposal and lap dancing. "Yes, Dad said that. In his words, I was lucky to be working at a large company like that with a Desmond. That's what he calls a 2:2. It's so unfair, though. Dad doesn't even have a degree, and nor does Mum. She started one, but gave it up when she got pregnant."

"That wasn't your mother we met at Rustica, was it? She didn't look like you."

"No, that's Dad's mid-life crisis girlfriend."

"I don't blame him," Ross grinned. "From what I saw of her, she's gorgeous."

Amy giggled. He'd had his nose down Deirdre's cleavage. "Behave," she said. "Dee is Dad's age. They knew each other at school."

"They were holding hands like teenagers," Ross said. "Your father looked like he'd done well for himself, and I don't mean pulling Dee. That was a Savile Row suit, I'm positive." He smirked. "I have a few myself. What sort of work does he do?"

Amy rolled her eyes. "It's really boring." Almost as tedious as actuarial work, she nearly said. "He's an IT troubleshooter for a bank. He can find out anything from an IT system. He describes himself as the bank's equivalent of GCHQ, which makes him sound a thousand times more exciting than he really is."

"Boring jobs pay the bills," Ross said.

She felt a pang of pity for him. That statement was tantamount to saying his life was over. He was only thirty or so. "I won't let myself get trapped," she said. "As soon as we're back in London, I'm looking for another job. I've had enough of being shouted at by Parveen."

"I'll help you," Ross said, to her astonishment. "I'll ask my friends if they know of anything."

"You mean the old boys' network?"

"If you want to call it that," Ross said dismissively. "Look, the champagne's all gone and we haven't even had our main courses yet. How about another bottle? You only live once."

The champagne perfectly complemented the lobster which Amy had ordered. She was suddenly ravenous, asking for both cheese and a pudding afterwards.

"I like to see a woman with an appetite," Ross said approvingly. He reached for her hand across the table, and held it. His touch was firm, his hand pleasantly cool. "It's been a long day," he said. "We should be gentle with each other."

Amy gazed into his eyes. "I hardly know you," she murmured.

"What is there to say?" Ross asked. "I went to boarding school, Cambridge University and Veritable Insurance. One institution after another. I wasn't an only child like you, but I might as well have been. I'm much younger than my sisters, and they weren't home much either. We were all sent away to school."

131

"How old were you, Ross?" Amy asked. She blinked away tears of sympathy. She couldn't avoid a deep sense of compassion for the innocent child Ross must have been, pushed inexorably onto a treadmill when he should have been at home with his family.

"Eight when I first went." His blue eyes were calm, entirely lacking in self-pity. "One either sinks or swims. You can guess which I chose."

He was stroking her hand now. "I know you think me cold, Amy. That's my outer shell, the façade I choose to present to the world. There's passion within, but I keep it well-buried." His eyes appealed to her. "I'm saying too much, I think. It must be the champagne talking."

"No," Amy said, flattered that he should choose to open his heart to her. "You can say anything you like. I'm your friend, Ross, you know that." Whatever their differences before, they had worked together as a team today. He'd not only arranged a lawyer to help her, he'd been genuinely shocked to hear about the sham marriage, Jeb and the two sinister strangers. They could trust each other.

Ross lifted her hand to his lips and kissed it softly, as if a moth had swept its wings across her skin. He was interrupted by the arrival of dessert, an indulgent chocolate confection. "Enjoy," he said.

Once the meal was over, Ross asked if Amy wanted to go to the bar.

"I'll go to my room," she said. "It's been a long day, as you say."

"I'll walk you up there." Ross placed a hand lightly on the small of her back. It was still there as the lift whisked them to their floor, and as she unlocked her door. "May I come in?" he asked.

She turned her face to his. For once, Ross was a picture of humility, his mouth quivering and his blue eyes pleading. During her year in London, she'd longed for a boyfriend, any man at all. Now, a handsome, rich young man was interested in her. True, he hadn't always behaved well, but today he'd explained why. He'd been attentive and kind. "Yes," Amy said simply. She should give him a chance.

132

As soon as they were alone in the room, he enveloped her in his arms and kissed her lips, gently at first and then with increasing passion. His tongue slid inside her mouth, probing the tip of hers. Amy flushed, overwhelmed by desire. Giddy with wine and Ross' kisses, she began to feel unsteady on her feet. Ross seemed to sense it. He manoeuvred her to the huge, king-size bed.

"Sit down," he said, his voice hoarse.

She let him guide her, accepting his kisses and the way her clothes seemed simply to slip off as he caressed her. Soon, she was lying naked on the bed and Ross, also naked, was stroking her shoulders, breasts and thighs.

"You've got quite a bush," he murmured, gently parting the lips where her thighs met.

"And is that a problem?" Amy asked dreamily, wondering for a fleeting moment if she really should have saved her lunch money for a wax last week.

"It just stops me doing some of the things I might like," Ross said, "but I can see from your eyes what you really want, and that's no problem at all."

She was admiring his toned, muscled body, and he'd noticed. Tentatively, she touched his groin, seeing he was larger than her other lovers. They'd hardly been a representative sample of the human race, she thought ruefully; she could count them on the fingers of one hand.

"I think I can satisfy you," Ross grinned. "Wait – are you on the pill, Amy? I thought not. Let me slip on a condom." He grabbed his trousers and reached into a pocket. Putting on the condom with ease, he was inside her in one deft movement.

Amy's previous boyfriends had been the same age as her; relatively inexperienced in the bedroom and keen to finish quickly. Ross, nearly a decade older, had a different technique: smooth and lingering. Amy gasped as he tantalised her again and again. After what seemed like hours, she screamed as a wave of pleasure coursed through her.

Ross kissed her mouth tenderly. He rifled his trouser pockets again, this time for his smartphone. "Forty five minutes," he said, in a self-satisfied tone. "I hoped I could do better for you than that, Amy. Would you let me try again?"

She nodded, lying back as he began to nibble her shoulders and breasts. Heat rose within her. Smiling, Ross donned another condom and concentrated on taking her to the peak of arousal once more.

He was so fit because he worked out every day, she supposed, drifting off to sleep after Ross had left.

Amy slept soundly, only waking when Ross phoned her at eight. "Want to join me for breakfast?" he asked. "I've been to the gym already."

Amy's heart was light and she hummed a tune as she showered. She'd misjudged Ross before, seeing only his spiky exterior rather than the warm heart within. It was incredible that her father's assumptions about them as a couple had become reality. Even in her wildest daydreams, she would never have considered it.

Although she raced through her make-up routine and dressed quickly, Ross had already eaten by the time she arrived at the restaurant.

"I ordered coffee for you," he said, folding his copy of the Financial Times.

"Thanks. This beats toast at Steelhouse Lane any day." Amy determined to make the most of the sumptuous hotel breakfast, choosing flaky croissants and strawberry jam. The coffee, dark and delicious, cut through the sweet jam and swept away any lurking remnants of sleepiness.

"So," Ross said, "we'll see Marty Bridges today."

Amy was relieved. It was vital to her to find Kat, both to resolve the police investigation into her sham marriage and to help her flatmate escape the men who threatened her. She'd hoped Ross would still give his support. "I'm so glad you want to track her down, even now," she said.

134

Ross stared at her. "Why wouldn't I? I want to take Kat to Thailand, after all."

Amy gawped back. "What about last night?"

"What about it?" His eyes were glacial. "We're not in a relationship, Amy. You said you were my friend, and that's all we are: friends with benefits."

Chapter 26 Charles

Charles nervously lit a cigarette. He puffed silently, standing alone as city workers strode purposefully to their offices around him. As the nicotine worked its charms, he mentally rehearsed the speech he would make to Alex. He wasn't looking forward to their meeting. With the bank about to collect millions from Bishopstoke if the Veritable acquisition took place, his boss wouldn't want to hear about any deal breakers.

He stubbed out the cigarette and went inside, still feeling like a condemned man walking towards his execution. Alex was on the phone, and waved him to one side.

"Got to wrap up now," he heard Alex say, and then, looking at Charles, "Can you find a meeting room while I finish?"

Typical, Charles thought. Planning anything in advance was an alien concept to Alex. He expected his minions to do his bidding at a moment's notice. Meeting space was at a premium too, with a deal in progress. Fortunately, Charles had many friends among the support staff thanks to his tendency to treat them like human beings. It was a habit that Alex and others had unaccountably failed to master, but it stood Charles in good stead. One of the directors was out all morning, and his secretary made his office available to Charles. She even brought coffee.

"I'll see you outside for a smoke," Charles said to her, as Alex looked askance at him.

"Down to business," Alex said, shutting the door. "What are their IT systems like?"

"Mostly good, but there are weaknesses," Charles said cautiously. "Their product pricing is flawed. They make the same charge to smokers and non-smokers alike for health insurance." He took a personal interest in such matters, and had idly checked while he was running system tests.

"What?" Alex's shock registered on his face. "That's ridiculous. Smokers are bound to make more claims on a policy, so their premiums should be more expensive."

"They're not, though." Charles had brought his laptop with him. "Look, if you ask for an online quote, you'll see."

They went through the screens, with Alex first claiming to be a smoker and then saying he wasn't. The same amount was quoted for both.

"Have you looked at the premium algorithms?" Alex asked.

"Yes, and they appear to be different," Charles said. "However, the code relating to smokers has been switched off."

"This could be good news," Alex said. "Bishopstoke may use it to secure a price reduction."

He didn't mention the possibility that Bishopstoke would walk away from the deal, and Charles judged it tactless to raise it. Instead, he listened as Alex made phone calls, first to the director who was leading Project Termite for the bank, and then to Bishopstoke's IT director.

"They want to escalate it," Alex said. "They're arranging a meeting with Davey Saxton urgently, and you'll have to come along. Can I suggest you remember who our client is? It's not your de facto brother-in-law, it's Bishopstoke, and I expect you to behave accordingly."

"You can rely on me," Charles said, inwardly seething at the attack on his professionalism. As soon as he could, he hurried outside for a calming cigarette.

A dozen men and one woman gathered in David Saxton's office an hour later. Among them were the IT directors of both Bishopstoke and Veritable, and Saxton's opposite number at Bishopstoke. This was Alana Green, a black American with a reputation for ruthlessness. Saxton could have remained seated at his desk, setting himself apart from the assembled company, but he had chosen to sit beside Alana at the meeting table. He was no longer the curly-haired scamp Charles remembered from their schooldays. Already balding in his early

137

forties, he nevertheless radiated energy and confidence. This was a man who was used to having his own way.

Charles was easily the most junior person among the movers and shakers around the table. "Great view, Davey," he said, admiring the picture window over the Thames.

"Of course, you haven't been here before, have you? I rarely have time to look at it," Saxton admitted.

Alex, his expression distinctly unfriendly, caught Charles' eye.

"Let's cut to the chase," Alana interjected. "I invited us all here because I understand there are major pricing issues with your products."

"Not major ones," Charles began to say.

Alex cut him off. "Yes, we discovered errors in health insurance pricing when we tested your systems. Obviously, we all need to touch base on that."

"You've done ten times as much business with smokers this year as last, but only because you underpriced their health insurance. There will be losses when the claims are paid. If we extrapolate across your product range, Veritable's profit forecasts look pretty sick," Alana said, a hint of her fabled aggression in her voice.

"You used a crucial word there: if. Maybe we can't, and don't even need to, extrapolate," David Saxton said. "I'd like to understand the problem better, and I suspect Charles can explain it to us. Do you want to go ahead, Charles?"

Charles outlined the facts he'd presented to Alex earlier. When he'd finished, everyone wanted to speak at once.

"Let's take comments in turn," David Saxton suggested. "I want my IT director's reaction first. Freddy?"

Freddy, a dapper young man of Asian extraction, sounded angry. "It's not an IT problem," he said. "We just heard that differential pricing for smokers was switched off, right? Only two administrators have the power to do so, and I've checked who they are while he's been speaking."

138

"Who are they?" Saxton asked, his face grim. "I want to see them here, right away."

"The Actuarial Director and the Health Actuary," Freddy said.

"Cari Harrison and Ross Pritchard," Saxton translated. He jabbed at his phone. "Layla?" he said. "Tell Cari Harrison and Ross Pritchard to come along to my office immediately. Haul them out of meetings if you have to, please. Oh, Ross is away? Of course he is. Just Cari, then." He nodded to Alana. "Let's take a break until she arrives, shall we?"

Cari joined them seemingly within seconds. A short, slight woman with a bright red pixie cut, she marched briskly into Saxton's office. "I don't think I've been introduced to everyone, Davey," she beamed, looking around.

David Saxton reeled off a list of everyone's name, company and job title. Charles was impressed. He was sure Saxton hadn't met most of them until half an hour before.

"So, Cari," Saxton said, "we know you're a busy woman, and we'll keep this brief. Health insurance sales have rocketed this year."

"Yes, we've taken the market by storm," Cari agreed. "I introduced a new pricing algorithm and that really helped."

"On that note, I'm afraid to say we may have underpriced our offering to smokers," Saxton said. "The code that differentiated them from non-smokers has been disabled by a system administrator."

Cari's eyes widened. "That's impossible," she breathed. "The only person who could do that is Ross Pritchard."

"And you," Freddy said drily.

"I wouldn't know where to start." Cari simpered. "IT isn't my forte at all."

"Could Ross have done this to any other products too?" Saxton asked.

"No, I don't think so," Cari said.

"I want to be sure," Saxton responded. "Freddy, please can you check pricing of every product for which Ross Pritchard has administrator status. Cari, I don't think we need you any longer today – please see HR at once and ask them to investigate Ross for gross misconduct." He waited until she'd left, then added, "I think that concludes the matter. It's a problem limited to the current year, and one product line only. There's no need to extrapolate."

Alana Green rolled her eyes. "An accomplished performance," she said. "She twisted you round her little finger. Smiling sweetly, batting her eyelashes, and making her subordinate carry the can."

Charles saw doubt in David Saxton's expression. He waited with bated breath for Saxton's reaction.

"Fine," Saxton replied. "Freddy will check if any other products, across our entire range, have been subject to administrator override. We will, of course, present you with full details of our findings, and you're welcome to audit them. Happy?"

"Delighted," Alana said.

Charles had always believed Americans incapable of irony. Alana Green had evidently worked in the UK for too long. She had gone native.

Chapter 27 Ross

Ross wished Amy would stop sulking. After the drama of the preceding day, they'd both needed R&R last night. She'd been as eager for it as he was. He'd been totally honest, making no false promises or declarations of love. What did she expect from a one night stand? He sighed. "Nearly there now. We just need to cross the main road."

"Easier said than done," Amy muttered.

It was a busy highway called Holloway Head. They had approached it from a quiet side street, although they heard the flow of traffic well before they had sight of it. Florence Street lay opposite them.

"How's your jaywalking?" Ross asked.

She glared at him. "The single time a taxi would be useful, you decide to walk," she complained. Eventually, the traffic eased just enough for them to dash across.

East West Bridges occupied an unlovely corrugated iron warehouse with a single storey brick office tacked onto the front, seemingly as an afterthought. To the side was a lumpy stretch of tarmac, on which were parked a few old, battered superminis and a shiny silver Jaguar with the number plate MJB 100. The office door was right next to the Jaguar. There was an illuminated buzzer, which Ross pressed.

A female voice, fuzzy with static, questioned them about their visit. The buzzer sounded to indicate the interrogator's satisfaction.

They were admitted to a small anteroom, shabby with chipped white paint and scuffed grey carpet tiles. It was empty apart from a couple of orange plastic chairs and a CCTV camera mounted near the ceiling. There was a white chipboard door leading to the offices beyond. Ross pushed it, to find it locked. "Welcome to Fort Knox," he said to a scowling Amy.

A middle-aged man, somewhat shorter than Ross, opened the door. "Marty Bridges," he said, advancing with a wide smile and his arm outstretched.

Ross shook his hand, noting Marty's strong grip. The man was obviously in his fifties, his white hair thinning rapidly, but his physique was still athletic. "I'm Ross Pritchard," he said. "This is my assistant, Amy Satterthwaite."

"Satterthwaite," Marty said, with a pronounced local accent. "Sit and wait. That's an unusual name, bab. I've not come across one of those before."

Amy glowered as Ross suppressed a chuckle.

Marty ushered them into a large office, as opulent as the anteroom was spartan. Apart from the lack of a Thames view, it would have served any of the Veritable directors. It was panelled in bird's eye maple, with a large polished desk and table made from the same wood. Marty pointed to black leather chairs clustered around the table. "Take a seat." He lifted his desk phone and speed-dialled a number. "Tanya, bring us some coffees will you, please? Thanks, angel." He sat at his desk, swivelling in a somewhat larger and more luxurious chair.

A dumpy, purple-haired woman of middle years brought a tray with a cafetière, three white china cups, cream and sugar. She nodded in response to Marty's thanks, leaving without a word.

Marty spooned three sugars into one of the cups. "Help yourself," he said, gesturing expansively. Once all the coffees were poured, he formed his hands into a steeple below his chin. "Tell me why you're here," he said.

"I have a business proposition as I said," Ross said. With a little thought, he had managed to fabricate a plausible excuse for the meeting. "I'm an actuary."

"Oh, bad luck," Marty said. "A job for someone who found accountancy too exciting. Tell me more."

"I want to set up a new niche insurance company, and I'm looking for funding."

"What's your track record?" Marty asked.

"A first from Oxbridge, a rowing blue and ten years at Veritable, during which I was rapidly promoted," Ross replied, handing Marty his business card.

"Veritable, indeed," Marty said. "My neighbour's daughter works there. Parveen. She's doing very well. Do you know her?"

Ross realised Amy wanted to speak. He kicked her under the table, just a gentle tap on her ankle. The last thing he needed was a rant from her about Parveen's shortcomings. "Yes, of course I know Parveen. She's quite a livewire," he said, as Amy simmered.

Marty chortled. "A good description," he said. "Parveen's a bright spark, right enough. Is she in on your project?"

"No, it's at an early stage," Ross said. "Before I bring anyone else on board, I need initial equity investment."

"I haven't got any for you," Marty said. "Not a sausage. Now, tell me why you're really here."

"I can share some projections with you," Ross said smoothly. Thanks to Cari, he was skilled at presenting an unruffled surface whilst panicking within.

"Don't give me that," Marty said, his expression suddenly wary. "I've been in business long enough to tell when someone's lying. I know who you really are. Lizzie Clements was attacked, and you're the couple they're looking for. Anyone can see you meet their descriptions. I could call the police and they'd nick you in an instant."

"We've seen the police already," Ross said, "and been cleared. Ring my lawyer and ask him if you like. The culprits are London villains."

"Londoners?" Marty said. "Why would they come here to thump an old lady?"

"They're looking for Kat," Amy blurted, "and so are we."

Marty raised an eyebrow. Ross prayed it would be the last interruption from Amy. It was proving hard enough to gain Marty's confidence. "You know Kat, don't you?" he said to Marty. "She's in

143

grave danger. The men who attacked Lizzie meant to kill her. They didn't succeed. They won't want to fail again."

Marty sipped his coffee in silence. "I don't understand," he said eventually. "What has Kat done to make anyone want to kill her?"

"She owes money," Amy chipped in.

Ross was surprised she didn't say more. As it happened, Marty nodded, apparently accepting her reply.

"I haven't seen Kat for years," Marty said. "Or Lizzie either. I sent flowers to the hospital as soon as I heard, of course. She was my housekeeper for many years. Prone to giving her opinion where it wasn't wanted, mind. That's why she's not working for me now. She couldn't half give it some lip, but she didn't deserve a battering."

"Nor does Kat," Ross said.

"It might help me make my mind up if you tell me who you are," Marty said curtly.

"I'm Kat's boyfriend and Amy's her flatmate," Ross said.

"Okay," Marty said slowly. "I think I will ring your lawyer if you don't mind. Who is he?"

"It's Ted Edwards of Edwards Margettson."

"I'll look him up online," Marty said. "I'm going to have to ask you to wait outside until I've phoned him."

Purple-haired Tanya was summoned to take Ross and Amy back to the lobby. "Would you like more coffee?" she offered.

Ross looked around the unprepossessing room, seeing nowhere for Tanya to leave a tray. He struggled to hide his exasperation. "I think not," he murmured.

It was a matter of minutes before Bridges returned, his face wreathed in smiles. "You're a jolly good chap, I hear," he said, in a passable imitation of the lawyer's refined vowels. "Come back to my office. Tanya's making another drink for you."

To Ross' relief, Bridges seemed much less guarded. "How do you think I can help?" the businessman asked, escorting them into his inner sanctum once more.

"Just tell us everything you can about Kat, her family and friends," Ross suggested.

Marty shrugged. "All right, Inspector Clouseau. There aren't many of them left, unfortunately. You know I was in partnership with her father?"

"Yes. A Russian, wasn't he?" Ross said, judging it inadvisable to say he'd learned this from Lizzie less than forty eight hours ago.

"Not from Russia itself, but one of the stans to the south. It doesn't make a lot of difference, I suppose. I met Sasha shortly after the Soviet Union broke up. I'd left school at sixteen, when there were no jobs here. Do you remember the slogan 'Labour isn't working?' It was an election poster, showing a dole queue stretching as far as the eye could see."

Despite his best efforts to be charming, Ross couldn't avoid a blank stare.

"No you don't, do you? You two are the same age as my kids. They've no idea either. At that time, there was a hellish recession in the Midlands. Rather than move to London, I set up my own business, buying and selling. It was slow at first, but with the fall of communism, I knew the east was a land of opportunity. I taught myself Russian and took a plane out there. Sasha managed a vodka factory. He wanted to turn it into a premium brand, so we worked on it together. The result was Snow Mountain."

Ross nodded. "That's good stuff."

"Well marketed," Amy said.

"You're both right," Marty grinned. "It was excellent quality, and we were ahead of the curve in selling it only to upmarket outlets. We both made good money. I built the rest of my business on the back of it. Look at this place. I started with nothing. And this isn't all. I've got fingers in more pies than I've had hot dinners. Maybe I could even consider an insurance start-up." He looked extremely smug. "Sasha did well enough to send his kids to boarding school here in England, which probably saved their lives. It all went pear-shaped when Sasha fell out with the government."

"What happened?" Again, Ross didn't care to admit that he'd heard part of the story before.

"They threw him in gaol. All his assets were confiscated and his wife, Maria, left penniless. She phoned me, and I sent her money – enough for her to live on, and to engage lawyers to fight Sasha's corner. They made it clear the officials wanted bribes." Marty shuddered. "This is between these four walls, but I paid them an absolute fortune. My business nearly went under."

"Why did you pay? You didn't have to. And it's against the law, isn't it?" Ross was surprised to hear such a story from a man who'd been described as hard-nosed.

"He was like a brother to me." Marty's blue eyes were troubled. "It was all for nothing," he said bitterly. "The secret police came for Maria. She and Sasha were never seen again. They died in prison." He laughed, a hollow sound. "Ironically, the bribes did me some good. They gave the factory to one of the President's strongest supporters, and he couldn't wait to do business with me. I wouldn't trust him as far as I could throw him, but together we've taken Snow Mountain global. It's a premium international brand."

"Great, everything ends happily ever after for you and Snow Mountain," Amy said. "What about Kat?"

"She was sixteen when her father died," Marty said. "I'd been funding her school fees for two years. She stayed with my family during the school holidays, even at Christmas. I helped her and her older brother with asylum claims. They're British citizens now. I did everything I could for them. She got a cob on. Told me it wasn't enough. I should have insisted that only Sasha could run the factory, apparently. As if anyone would have listened! Still, according to her, it was all my fault her parents died. She wanted nothing more to do with me. Half an hour later, she walked out of my house and I never saw her again."

Ross could tell Amy didn't believe Marty. He kicked her ankle again. She looked daggers at him.

"There you are," Marty said, catching Ross' eye. "I'll never understand feminine logic as long as I live. Anyway, Kat was capable of earning a living at sixteen. I had to, and my children didn't go to college either. The university of life: that's where we had our education."

"You fell out with Lizzie too," Amy pointed out.

"She's a cantankerous old bat," Marty replied.

"I don't have to listen to this misogyny," Amy said hotly. She stormed out of Marty's office.

"Who rattled the bab's cage?" Marty asked, with a ribald chuckle. "She needs a good seeing to, that one."

"I tried, and it didn't work," Ross said ruefully.

Marty winked.

"Cut her some slack, Marty. She's been through a lot. One of the criminals held a knife to her throat. Another ransacked her flat and stole a couple of plants." As he spoke, he was aware of how odd it sounded.

Marty's reaction was unexpected. "What did he look like?" the businessman asked, eyes serious.

Ross struggled to remember what Amy had said. "You'll have to ask her," he said finally.

"She won't have gone far." Marty left his office, returning a few minutes later with a sheepish-looking Amy. "She ended up getting lost in my warehouse," he explained.

"Amy," Ross said, "Marty's told us what he knows, and it's only fair we do the same for him. Can you give him a description of your visitors?"

She knew immediately which visitors he meant. "There were two," she said. "The first was the man who searched Kat's room and took two pot plants. He was tall and skinny. Green eyes, long nose, spiky black hair, scruffy."

Marty laughed. "That would be Erik, Kat's brother. Wouldn't hurt a fly. You don't need to worry about him."

That could be a promising avenue to explore. "Can you give me his contact details?" Ross asked.

"Sorry, I can't," Marty said. "I told you, I haven't seen Kat for years. Anyway, that was one visitor. What about the other?"

Amy described the knifeman.

"That's interesting," Marty mused. "Londoner, was he?"

"Yes," she said.

"He was here yesterday. A couple of cockneys dropped by, after a crate of Snow Mountain. That guy and a black thug."

"Was he light-skinned, with a nose ring and single earring?" Amy asked.

Marty nodded.

Amy looked at Ross. "That was Jeb," she said. "Kat thinks he's her friend."

"He's a killer," Ross said. "They're dangerous men, Marty."

"I can look after myself. Let me show you something." Marty reached into a drawer in the bird's eye maple desk, and pulled out a can of pepper spray and a sheaf of boxing certificates. "Those guys thought they could threaten me yesterday, and I didn't appreciate that. They won't be back."

Chapter 28 Marty

Marty shook his head, watching the ill-matched pair from his window. They were walking back to the Malmaison, they'd said. Were they really who they seemed? The lawyer seemed to think so.

He phoned Erik. "I've just had a visit from Kat's boyfriend and her flatmate," he said. "Allegedly."

"I've met a flatmate," Erik said. "Amy. Tall, ginger hair, nervous."

"Hot temper?" Marty asked.

"Oh, yes," Erik said. "Snapped at me like a crocodile when I visited their flat."

Marty laughed. "I got a taste of that when she dropped in today. There was a boyfriend, too: Ross. What do you know about him?"

"Kat hasn't mentioned him."

Marty shrugged. He wondered how serious Ross and Kat's relationship was anyway. The man didn't think twice about sleeping with her flatmate. "Did she talk about a couple of Cockneys – a lad called Jeb, and an older guy?"

"Never. We don't discuss her private life."

Why was he now suspecting Erik of dissembling, Marty mused. He'd always found Erik straight as a die, yet there was an odd note in his voice.

"I think she's in trouble," Marty said. "You know Lizzie was attacked and left for dead?"

"I didn't." Erik sounded shocked.

"The flatmate and the boyfriend say it was the other two who did it, and they'll be doing the same to Kat when they find her." He paused. "Wherever your sister is, and whatever she's done, she should go to the police. You'll have to tell her."

"I will," Erik said, and this time, Marty wholeheartedly believed him.

149

Chapter 29 Amy

"What do you think he did to Jeb?" Amy asked Ross as they walked away from East West Bridges. She remained furious, both with herself and with him. They still needed to work as a team, though. She'd seen Ross' face when Marty refused to say where Erik was. It mirrored her own disappointment.

"Gave him a black eye, I hope. Jeb certainly deserved it," Ross replied. "Why would Jeb pretend to be interested in vodka, though? It doesn't stack up."

"Marty didn't help him," Amy said.

"He wouldn't help us either," Ross said. "We're running out of options."

He seemed so dejected that she was tempted to hug him, but good sense prevailed. She wanted no further physical contact with Ross, in the bedroom or anywhere else.

They crossed Holloway Head, this time without difficulty. With no more ideas to share, they walked together without speaking until the silence was broken by a call on Ross' phone.

She could tell it was serious because he turned white as a sheet. "It's a joke, isn't it?" she heard him say.

When he finished, his face was strained. "That was HR," he said.

"How did they know I was with you?" Amy asked. She hated her job, but even so, it was better than nothing. After being sacked for faking sickness, she would struggle to find any work at all.

Ross gazed at her with blank incomprehension. "They didn't mention you," he said. "I've been summoned back to London on suspicion of gross misconduct. If I don't see HR this afternoon to help with their investigation, I'll be fired."

"That's unbelievable," Amy murmured, her jaw dropping.

"Even worse," Ross said, "it was a junior HR manager, not the director."

"What do you mean?" She was bemused.

"If they're giving me the monkey rather than the organ-grinder, it means they've made up their minds," Ross said bitterly. "At least if the police suspect you of a crime, you're entitled to a lawyer and a fair investigation, as we know. Once HR have you in their sights, they're police, judge, jury and executioner combined."

"But what have you done? You didn't throw a sickie."

"I did nothing wrong, I assure you," Ross said. "But I've been accused of a computer fraud. It's been alleged that I deliberately mispriced health insurance to increase sales and receive a huge bonus." He sighed. "I'm going straight to the station and back to London now. Stay here, Amy. I'll be back tonight. Whatever happens, whether I lose my job or not, I'm going to find Kat."

She threw caution to the winds and flung her arms around him as they reached the Malmaison. He stroked her hair, and she felt her treacherous senses come alive. Tearing herself away, she watched him walk through the underpass that led to the station, until he disappeared from view. He had to be innocent. With a lump in her throat, she realised she couldn't help, but at least she knew someone who could.

Chapter 30 Charles

Charles was surprised to receive a phone call from Amy at work, and rather taken aback when she asked if he was busy.

"Fairly," he said cautiously. "I could meet you after work for an hour if you like."

"That won't be necessary," Amy said, "nor is it practical. I'm in Birmingham."

"What are you doing there?"

"Ross brought me here for a few days," Amy said. "We're having a break at the Malmaison hotel. It's great for shopping."

"He does seem a pleasant young man," Charles said.

"Oh, he is," his daughter said; tenderly, Charles thought. "He has a bit of an IT problem, though, and I wanted your advice. You're a computer expert, aren't you?"

"I like to think so," Charles said with pride.

"Great. Well, Ross has been accused of misusing his computer access at work to change the price of health insurance. He didn't do it, Dad, but how can he prove it?"

She had run to him with skinned knees as a child, and now she still turned to Charles when she found a problem insoluble. If only he could kiss it better as he used to. He fell silent as he recalled the meeting in Davey's office. Of course, Cari had blamed the fraud on Ross Pritchard, who was absent. Why hadn't Charles realised it was his daughter's boyfriend who was being accused? Although the investigation was an internal matter for Veritable, he could have offered help to find the culprit. It wasn't too late for that. He resolved to suggest it to Alex immediately.

"Dad?" Amy asked. "Are you still there?"

"Yes," Charles said. "I'll think about it and let you know." He couldn't breathe a word to her about Project Termite.

"When?" she asked. The disappointment in her voice was palpable.

"By tomorrow," he promised.

"Please be as quick as you can," she pleaded.

"I will." He said goodbye with a heavy heart. A cigarette had never held greater appeal, despite the blinding summer heat outside.

Equilibrium restored, Charles found Alex about to leave for lunch.

"You want to run further diagnostics on their health products?" Alex said. "No way. That's boiling the ocean."

"I don't think it's a waste of time at all," Charles said, deliberately substituting plain English for Alex's management jargon. "The sooner Veritable know who was responsible for the fraud, the sooner they can fix it."

"Who cares?" Alex said icily. "Bishopstoke will fire Veritable's A to C suites anyway. That's how they'll deliver synergies to the market. The control weaknesses you found just give Bishopstoke more leverage. I don't want you to do any more analysis. Bishopstoke already have all the ammunition they need." He looked at the clock. "I'm late for my lunch appointment. Must go."

Charles grappled with his dilemma. He generally used his discretion to complete tasks in the least time possible. It was unusual for him to volunteer for extra work, and certainly not to carry out duties he'd been expressly forbidden to perform. Nevertheless, his daughter's happiness was paramount. Sighing, he decided to go for a stroll at lunchtime. He often resorted to smoking when he needed to reflect. It wasn't the nicotine that helped him solve problems, he suspected, but the effect of being alone with his thoughts.

He walked down to the river. The suffocating heat of morning was easing, a light breeze ruffling the water's shimmering surface. Pleasure boat trippers waved to him. Charles ignored them, brushing away the droplets of spray blown in his direction.

He no longer had access to Veritable's IT system, but Davey Saxton did, or at any rate could arrange it for Charles. Davey, his old schoolmate and Deirdre's brother, was probably the only FTSE100 chief executive who would readily take a phone call from him. Why

153

shouldn't Charles pop round after work and run the diagnostics? It was a private matter; almost within the family. Charles retrieved his smartphone from his pocket and began to dial.

Chapter 31 Ross

Ross had always made a point of being civil to Veritable's HR director, Carolina Tait. Carolina's minions were a different matter. They were part of the vast majority of individuals at the company whose existence he barely acknowledged. Unless they were well-established in Veritable's hierarchy, he would blank them at the coffee machine, in meetings, at the Christmas party and at the glass gates where he swiped his smartcard to gain access to the office. It was here that his plight really hit home. His card simply refused to work.

The uniformed security man's badge gave his name as Conrad. Ross wasn't sure if Conrad was new to the company or had been there for ten years. Like many of his colleagues, the man was little more than wallpaper to the high-flying actuary. "You, Conrad – can you help?" Ross asked impatiently.

Conrad tried swiping the card. "It's out of date," he told Ross.

"They're supposed to last forever," Ross complained.

"Not if you've left the company's employment, Sir," Conrad said.

"Of course I haven't," Ross spluttered. "Ask Joanne Tonks. I'm supposed to be having a meeting with her."

"What's the name, Sir?"

"Ross Pritchard. Can't you tell from the card?"

"Very good, Sir."

Conrad ambled slowly to the reception desk. Ross saw him pick up the phone and speak for a while.

"I've left a message for her, Sir," Conrad said.

"Aren't you going to let me in?" Ross asked.

Conrad stood still by the gate, sturdy and immovable. "Please sign in at reception and we'll give you a visitor's pass, Sir."

Ross did as he was bid, and was directed to sit on one of the uncomfortable black leather sofas reserved for visitors. A pristine copy of the Financial Times, obviously unread, lay on a coffee table in front of him. Ross flicked through its pages.

A trio of chatty blondes, about Amy's age, clattered through the revolving door in noisy stilettos. They made their way past Ross to Conrad's gate.

"Late lunch was it, girls?" Conrad said, leering at the most buxom of the three.

"Poets Day, Conrad," she replied, and they all laughed.

"You've got a visitor, Jo," Conrad said, jerking his thumb at Ross.

"I'll call him when I'm ready. Got to find Cari Harrison first," she told him. Without a backward glance, the three girls slipped through the glass gates.

Chapter 32 Amy

There was nothing to be done but wait – for Ross to return with news about his summons to London, for her father to use his black art to prove Ross was innocent, even for Marty to change his mind about helping them. She doubted somehow that any of those things would happen, so most of all, Amy waited for a stroke of luck.

Every avenue they'd explored in the search for Kat had led nowhere. Maybe the police would find her, and if so, Amy wished fervently it would be before Jeb and the knifeman. She sat in shade under a café canopy, sipping chilled wine and trying to enjoy the scene before her.

She had found a café bar behind the Malmaison, overlooking a canal. The water sparkled silver in the sunlight. Squinting, she saw an arched bridge in the distance, a jetty, and a cluster of houseboats painted in bright colours like a flower garden.

Amy fidgeted restlessly and ordered more wine. She could afford a treat, just. Ross had paid for everything since they left her flat two days before. Anyway, the wine was delicious, and well-priced compared with Fitzrovia. Her second glass softened her tension and unease.

As she relaxed at last, her phone began to play Michael Jackson's Thriller. It was her father.

"Good news, Amy," he said.

"Really?" She could scarcely contain her excitement. "You've proved he didn't do it?"

"Hardly," Charles said.

She looked longingly at the wine. Could she take a gulp without him hearing it? "You said it was good news," she accused.

"It is," Charles replied. "I haven't run diagnostics on Veritable's systems – in fact, I didn't even need to ask for access – because their IT team had done it already. I phoned Davey Saxton, only to discover they were already on the case."

157

"So they know it wasn't Ross?"

"Yes," Charles said. "That's about the size of it."

Amy didn't press him for more. She was eager to tell Ross. When she dialled, however, she was immediately diverted to his voicemail message. 'Hello, it's Ross here. I'm very busy but will ring you back at the earliest possible opportunity.'

He could be so pompous, she thought. Smiling, she left a message, noting that another call was waiting.

The caller withheld his number. As soon as he spoke, she knew it wasn't Ross. Nevertheless, the voice was familiar.

"It's Erik. Remember?" It was the tall, thin man who'd removed Kat's plants from their flat.

Amy recalled how careful he'd been not to introduce himself. She hadn't been sure whether he was friend or foe. Marty had been emphatic, however: 'He wouldn't hurt a fly.'

"Erik, I have to see you again. Where are you?" she asked.

"In Birmingham, near the centre."

"Give me the address," she said eagerly. "I'll get over there as soon as I can." She couldn't afford to wait for Ross. Instead, she phoned him, suffered his recorded message again, and left details of what she was doing and where she was going.

Amy could have walked, but such was her excitement, she hailed a cab outside the hotel. Within minutes, it was stuck in a traffic jam.

"The council's working on the roads, like they do every summer," the driver said gloomily. "It'd be quicker to walk."

"I would, but I don't know the way."

He gave her directions and declined to take a fare from her. "I like to help a pretty girl out," he said, a small act of kindness that boosted her confidence after Ross' brutal rejection at breakfast.

The newer glass and concrete offices of the city centre soon gave way to old red brick buildings, elaborately ornamented and turreted in the gothic style. 'If you get lost, follow signs for the Big Peg,' the taxi driver had said, and she did, while having no idea what the Big Peg was. They led her past a white church in a leafy square, buzzing bars and jewellery workshops. She was looking for Leopold Passage, a pedestrian alleyway behind a badge factory. Amy almost missed it. It was nothing more than a narrow, cobbled path, winding steeply to the left, flanked on either side by the walls of buildings three storeys higher or more. Very occasionally, a narrow door or barred window punctuated the red brick. The effect was claustrophobic, like walking between cliffs.

Erik had told her to look for a door marked Clissolds. The path took another abrupt twist into a paved courtyard, and there it was, black-painted below a gothic arch. On either side of it were the two shrubs removed from Kat's room, each in a terracotta pot and the picture of health, greener and glossier than before. It was proof, if Amy needed it, that she'd found Kat's brother. But where was Kat?

Chapter 33 Shaun

Shaun was unimpressed by Marty Bridges' property portfolio. Although well located near busy highways roaring around Birmingham city centre, the sites were mostly undeveloped: scrapyards and stony car parks. Even at two pounds a day, Shaun wasn't tempted to risk his Merc's suspension.

"Why can't we just torch his warehouse?" Jeb whined.

"I told you before. Too many cameras," Shaun said, almost immediately having a subtle change of heart. Jeb was irritating him. The younger man was jumpy and smoking more than usual, probably taking too much cocaine again. Shaun decided he needed time alone. "I'll drop you off in Florence Street," he said. "See if you can find an angle out of sight of the CCTV."

It was possible that Jeb would succeed, and if not, it gave Shaun an hour or so to enjoy a peaceful pint.

Having left Jeb round the corner from East West Bridges, Shaun set his satnav to direct him to Hockley. This seemed more promising. Where previously he'd toured a hinterland of shabby factories and derelict sites, now he was in an area that had been gentrified. He drove through grand streets of tall, red brick buildings, often adorned with columns and curlicues in the same material. Occupied by jewellery tradesmen, design agencies and an occasional flat conversion, they were generally in a good state of repair. Losing a property here would hit Marty Bridges' pocket.

Shaun reversed into a parking space and fumbled in his pocket for change as he walked to the pay and display machine. His car had been acquired in payment for services rendered, and he was aware the supplier had stolen it and changed the number plate. Prudently, he preferred to park legally. It avoided drawing attention to his fake plate and lack of insurance and road tax.

He saw her then, on the other side of the road: Kat's flatmate, Amy. A nervous tic played at the corner of his mouth. She must know where Kat was. For a moment, he looked around for a traffic warden. He hadn't bought his ticket yet. Was there time to run across for a little chat with Amy? Although it was broad daylight, he could still secure her co-operation with a well-placed blade.

In the instant he looked away from her, a matter of a few seconds or so, Amy disappeared.

Shaun gawped. Doubt flooded him. While he didn't believe in ghosts, he wondered if she'd been simply a figment of his imagination. He fingered his chin, wincing as he touched the bruises Bridges had given him. Hidden by stubble, they were still tender. The pain brought him to his senses. He realised that, although the buildings across the road appeared to be a continuous terrace, they were not. A cobbled alley ran between them, a battered road sign stating that it was called Leopold Passage.

It sounded familiar. Shaun paid for his parking and checked the address of Marty Bridges' property: 3, Leopold Passage. Now he was not only sure where Amy had gone, he was certain he would find Kat there. Would Marty Bridges be there too? Shaun wasn't going to take any chances. He wanted Jeb with him, and they needed to tool up. He took out his phone.

Chapter 34 Amy

Amy pressed the large, old-fashioned cream ceramic doorbell. Although she heard no sound, the black door immediately opened, fractionally at first, then wider. Erik stepped out.

"Amy," Erik said, making an attempt at a smile. He still looked grave, his green eyes piercing hers. "Please come in." He ushered her over the threshold.

She found herself alone with him in a shabby corridor, barely decorated with peeling white paint. There was a pink plush carpet which appeared to have been roughly hacked to fit the space available. Ahead, bare wooden stairs led upwards. To either side was a panelled oak door. Erik pushed open the left hand one, revealing a large living space with a sofa and other furniture. Everything was of good quality but mismatched. The pink carpet in this room did not quite stretch as far as the walls, revealing grey lino in the gaps. A blanket covered the front window, extinguishing any stray shafts of sunlight that might have filtered into the courtyard outside. Above, a bare light bulb illuminated the room.

"It's not homely like your flat," he apologised.

"It's ten times as large," Amy said. It was as clean and tidy too. As in Kat's room in Fitzrovia, books were neatly stacked on shelves free of dust, and cut flowers arranged in a vase. She scrutinised Erik. Looking closer now, she noticed the family resemblance. He had Kat's green eyes and slightly long nose. Even so, she could see from the lines at his mouth and forehead that he had a different personality from his sister. Erik was watchful and serious where Kat was happy-go-lucky.

"Do you take tea?" Erik asked. "It's all I can offer you, I'm afraid. I was about to make a cup for Kat."

"Where is she?" Amy asked.

Erik pointed to the ceiling. "She has a room upstairs. I rent the whole property from Marty Bridges, so there's more than enough space for both of us."

"Marty?" Amy was stunned. "He said he hadn't seen you for years."

Erik grinned. "He may have told you he hadn't seen Kat for years. He certainly doesn't know she's here. But he would suspect she and I were in contact, I believe." He added, "Marty called me earlier with a long story about Kat being chased by gangsters – and also by you."

"I need to warn her," Amy said. "Please let me see her."

"When we've talked," Erik replied. "I can warn her if I have to. But I want to understand first why she's running away and won't talk to the police."

"Marty's told you Kat's in danger," Amy said. "Do you appreciate how much? She knows a man called Jeb. He tried to murder Lizzie Clements, and he'll kill Kat if he can. She owes his friends money." Amy didn't want to say more. She only had the knifeman's word that Kat was a thief. "We've got to call the police," she finished.

"That's the last thing my sister wants to do," Erik said. "According to her, Jeb is a friend who helped her out when she needed money. I'm not so sure. There were strings attached."

"Like marrying illegal immigrants?"

"Precisely," Erik said. "She has admitted to that. Jeb gave her a thousand pounds a time. I understand the police will take a dim view, although I don't see why they should care. It's a victimless crime. She's staying here until she works out what to do."

"Hardly victimless, Erik. Kat stole my identity to marry one of them," Amy retorted.

"That, she did not say." His green eyes were kind, concerned. "You think Jeb is a murderer," he said. "What makes you so sure?"

"Almost too much," Amy replied. "They found a knife with Jeb's fingerprint in Lizzie Clements' flat. A friend of his held a knife to my

163

throat in London and came looking for Kat here. These people live in a darker world than you or I." She remembered then that his parents had died in a foreign prison, and regretted her words.

"You must persuade my sister," Erik said.

They heard footsteps and Kat waltzed into the room, looking as glamorous and carefree as ever. She was wearing a jade silk kimono, a garment Amy had often seen when they both rose languorously on a Saturday morning. "It's so lovely to see you, Amy," she breathed, air-kissing Amy in a cloud of perfume.

"Kat," Erik said, "you must listen to Amy. She has bad news about Lizzie, and Jeb is involved. Also, if what Amy says is true, you have abused her trust and you owe her an apology." He glanced at his sister expectantly.

"I didn't think it was illegal to marry someone," Kat said.

"But to use another woman's name?" Erik asked.

Kat shrugged. "Surely it isn't a big deal? You weren't going to marry anyone else soon."

Momentarily, Amy was lost for words. "Nor was Bronwen, I suppose," she said, seeing from Kat's eyes that she was right.

Kat clearly realised she'd overstepped the mark. "Amy, we're all young girls," she said hastily, "enjoying ourselves before we settle down. Who says any of us are the marrying kind?"

Their conversation was interrupted by the strains of Thriller deep within Amy's handbag. She fished out the phone, and saw it was Ross calling.

Chapter 35 Ross

Allowed through Veritable's glass gates after stewing in the lobby for ten minutes, Ross had a very short meeting with Joanne Tonks. She'd hardly had time to usher him into one of the seminar rooms overlooking the river before Carolina Tait burst anxiously into the room. There had been some IT problems, according to Carolina; mistakes had been made, and she was deeply sorry he'd been disturbed on holiday. Ross accepted the HR director's grovelling apology without a fuss. Noticing a missed call from Amy, he didn't wish to linger at the office. He was already listening to her message as Conrad waved him back through the gates.

There was a taxi rank a few metres away. Ross jumped in a cab. "Can you get me to Birmingham fast?" he demanded, waving a fistful of banknotes.

The driver grimaced. "Only by taking you to Euston station," he volunteered. "The drive's over two hours. It's quicker by train."

Ross was in luck. He arrived at Euston just before a train was due to leave. Sprinting and jostling through the crowds, he caught it with seconds to spare. He immediately phoned Amy to let her know.

"That's wonderful news, and I've got some too." Amy sounded excited. "I'm with Kat right now."

"Where?" Ross asked. "Leopold Passage?" He couldn't quite believe it.

"Yes," she said, warning him, "The traffic was dreadful earlier. You'll have to walk here, but it's actually not far from the station."

He overheard a man say it was a fifteen minute walk. "Who's that?" Ross asked. "Erik?"

Amy confirmed it was. "How was your meeting?"

"HR made a mistake," he told her, resolving to find out more from Carolina one day. It did no harm to be gracious towards Carolina; he might need her goodwill in future.

"Ross…" Amy evidently didn't care much about his spat with HR, for she changed the subject swiftly. "Erik's flat isn't that easy to find. You'd miss the passage if you weren't looking for it."

Ross dismissed her concerns, but just in case, opened a map on his iPad as soon as the call was over. Exhilaration flowed through him. At last, he would see Kat again. He spent a pleasant journey browsing the internet for five star hotels in Thailand. Energy levels high, he leaped off the train as soon as its doors opened, and ran: through Birmingham's central shopping streets, the business district with its lawyers' offices and pubs, then finally into the grid of Victorian streets that comprised the Jewellery Quarter. He slowed as he approached Leopold Passage, hearing voices in the cobbled alleyway.

"You took your time," he heard a man say, with an evident London twang. There was a gruff, but indistinct, reply.

Ross tiptoed cautiously into the passage, following its twists and turns until he reached the courtyard. The duo standing in front of the black door had their backs to him, but he knew them immediately from Amy and Marty's descriptions: Shaun, clearly the elder, a touch of grey in his hair; and taller, darker Jeb.

Ross' first thought was to call the police. He took his phone from his pocket, preparing to run to safety as he dialled 999.

"Where do you think you're going?" Shaun spun round.

"I'm looking for the station," Ross said, a poor effort at bluffing and clearly a wasted one. Shaun's eyes held a glint of recognition. The criminal undoubtedly recalled their encounter in the pub.

"Yeah, right," Shaun said, rushing at Ross and knocking his phone to the ground. It shattered on the hard cobbles, shards of glass and silvery plastic shining in the sun.

Ross ducked as Shaun swung a fist at his face. While hardly a streetfighter, he had learned to hold his own at boarding school.

The door opened. Another man emerged and promptly head-butted Jeb. Momentarily distracted, Ross allowed Shaun to land a punch on his throat. He staggered, winded, as Shaun rained blows to his head, jaw and chest.

"Get inside, Ross." The newcomer, skinny, black-haired and green-eyed, was grappling with Shaun, Jeb now being preoccupied with a bloodied nose. This must be Erik, Ross realised.

"Got to stop them," Ross panted.

"No," Erik said, temporarily disabling Shaun with a kick to the groin. "You must help my sister. She'll know where to go."

Ross heard Kat scream. He needed no further urging.

Chapter 36 Jeb

"Shoot him, Shaun," Jeb pleaded. He would have done it himself without a second thought if he hadn't been occupied in staunching the flow of blood from his nose. Wrath bubbled inside him, a cauldron of hate about to spill. It had been a trying day.

"No. Too noisy," Shaun said, ducking as Erik took a swing at him.

Jeb scanned the courtyard quickly. Other buildings had windows overlooking it. Grudgingly, he conceded that Shaun was right. While Kat's screams hadn't attracted attention yet, it was foolhardy to invite it. Trembling with rage, he took his right hand away from his bloodied face, reaching inside his sock for a silent weapon.

Erik was absorbed in his fist fight with Shaun, having evidently decided Jeb posed no further threat to him. That was a big mistake.

The flick-knife slipped swiftly out of Jeb's sock, where it had lain flush against his heel, and into the palm of his right hand. He waited for Erik to stay steady for a few seconds. If that meant his boss was thumped another couple of times first, too bad. Shaun was hard enough. He'd forget as long as Jeb delivered results.

Jeb flicked the blade open. It glittered in the sunshine. Jeb noticed Erik focus on it, but too late. With a single deft swipe, Jeb cut the man's throat from ear to ear.

"Nice one, Jeb," Shaun said approvingly.

Jeb grinned. His anger was dissipating in the pride of a job well done. Adrenaline coursed through him now. His quarry was near. It was imperative to kill Kat before she could tell Shaun the truth.

He set his cigarette lighter aflame, and applied it to one of the glossy shrubs flanking the doorway. The plant's woody stem began to scorch, acrid smoke rising. Jeb chuckled with excitement. "Let's set the place on fire," he said.

Chapter 37 Amy

Kat screamed, a sound that spoke of far more than fear. "That was Shaun," she sobbed to Amy. "His eyes…I've never seen such cold fury."

To Amy, who'd already experienced Shaun's scary side, it was horribly believable. "We must call the police," she urged.

Kat stared at her. "We can run to safety. I know how."

"What about Erik? He's out there with Shaun and Jeb. They'll stop at nothing." Amy was appalled that Kat would abandon her brother to his fate. She would have pressed the point, had Ross not chosen that moment to burst through the front door.

"Kat, I heard you scream. Are you all right?" he asked, enveloping her in a hug.

Kat made no effort to extricate herself from his embrace. "We have to run away, Ross," she said, her eyes refilling with tears. She had the presence of mind to kick the door shut, though, Amy noted.

Beautiful despite her reddened eyes, Kat seemed to mesmerise Ross. He simply nodded.

"Erik told me we can escape through the cellar," Kat said. "There are tunnels below that can take us miles away." She led Ross by the hand to a door to the right of the stairs. "Amy – you're coming with us, aren't you? I want to be sure you're safe."

Kat's plea to Amy's loyalty succeeded. Amy followed the pair, helping them locate the light switch just inside the door. A single naked light bulb above revealed brick steps stretching downwards as the cellar door slammed shut behind the three of them.

There was no switch inside the cellar itself, though. Only the dimming rays of the bulb above the stairs gave illumination to the racking at the rear of the room.

"How do we get behind that?" she asked.

"Wriggle through," Ross said. "I'm serious. Amy – you first, then Kat. Use your smartphone as a torch. We have to get away from those thugs, and we're on our own. We can't even call the police now."

Kat's eyes glittered. "Good."

Ross raised an eyebrow. "You've got nothing to fear," he said loyally. "Whatever that killer made you do, it was under duress. They'll never prosecute you."

Amy knelt down in the dust and scrambled into the racking. It was easier than it looked. Ross was still explaining to Kat she could have faith in British justice, his lawyer friends would easily win a case even if it were brought to trial, which he doubted. Kat made protesting noises. Couldn't Ross see why Kat didn't trust the law? The poor girl's parents had died in a foreign gaol. "Help Kat get through the door," she called.

Behind the door, a rush of cool air hit Amy's cheeks; pleasant after the stickiness of the summer's day above. A spiral metal ladder descended into gloom. Holding her precious torch carefully, Amy made her way down. While the rungs were evenly spaced, the final step onto solid earth was not. Amy landed awkwardly.

The jarring impact loosened her grip on the phone. It fell to the ground and the light from it disappeared. Worse, pain shot through her left foot. "I've sprained my ankle," Amy gasped.

Ross' voice, above her, was remarkably free from panic. "You've probably just twisted it. Try putting some weight on it. Hold the ladder just in case."

"It'll hurt," Amy protested.

"What do you think those thugs intend? I assure you that will hurt more," Ross said coldly. "I speak from personal experience."

Gingerly, she stepped from side to side. "I can hobble," she reported.

"It's nothing serious then," Ross said. "Do you think you can find that phone before one of us treads on it? Kat and I will wait on the ladder until you do."

170

"We must get moving," Kat pleaded.

"We need light for that," Ross reminded her. "I don't want you to trip. Has your phone got a flashlight, Kat?"

"It's upstairs."

Amy shuffled cautiously from side to side, her ankle throbbing, until the tip of her left foot struck a small object. Reaching down, she found her phone, thankfully intact.

Its light revealed an imposing metal door, a circular combination lock inset opposite the hinges.

"One, two, three," Kat hissed.

Amy turned the dial to the numbers, just in time, for the door at the top of the shaft creaked open again. Her heart stopped. If it had been Erik, if by some miracle he had fought off the two brutes, he would have shouted the news. Most of all, he'd want to reassure his sister. The silence meant Shaun and Jeb were inside the flat, and Erik was no longer fighting them. Amy could imagine the implications. She tried not to.

The huge grey block of metal swung open as soon as she'd entered the sequence. "Quick," she said, pushing Ross and Kat through, before slamming the door shut.

"We're safe now," Kat said.

Amy wasn't sure. Disorientated, she looked around. She'd feared the worst, expecting a descent into sewers, or a dank culvert for one of the canals that criss-crossed the city. Nothing had prepared her for the brightly-lit space in which she found herself. It was like a white-painted railway arch, with industrial cabling and lights strung at its apex. It wasn't so much a room as a huge corridor, easily wide enough for the trio to stand abreast. At one end was a brick wall, punctuated by the door through which she'd arrived. At the other end, the arch opened into a larger area.

The fluorescent lighting threw Ross' bruises and scratches into stark relief. Kat traced a finger across them, her face a picture of concern. "What did they do to you?" she murmured.

171

"Nothing much," Ross said.

"I thought Jeb was my friend," she said.

"I hope you know better now," he replied. His eyes flicked about the room. "I wonder what we've stumbled into. Look, this place is in impeccable order. It's clean and well-lit. If you listen," he cocked his ear, "you can hear machinery in the background. There must be other people around, and definitely another way out."

"Erik says this is a telecoms network," Kat told him. "There are several entrances."

"I knew it," Ross said. "No one else would crawl through a dusty cellar in the middle of nowhere. Now we've got away, let's find help – or at least, another exit." He took Kat's hand and began marching.

Amy hobbled behind as best she could, using the wall for support. Her ankle felt worse with every step. "Hang on," she called, seeing the pair turn left at the end of the room, "I can't keep up."

"We'll wait," Ross' disembodied voice said. As she turned the corner, he added, "I'll take your right shoulder and Kat can take the left. We're in this together."

Amy was grateful for his strength. He practically lifted her off the ground single-handed, so Kat and indeed Amy herself were bearing very little weight. There was no doubt that their combined pace was slower than his would have been alone, though.

They approached a fork in the corridor. "Listen," Ross said. "Those are voices in the distance, aren't they? Help is at hand."

"Far from it," Kat said, sudden terror in her eyes. "It's Jeb and Shaun."

Amy shared her fear. Shaun's visit to the flat had been frightening enough, but nothing compared with Lizzie's ordeal at Jeb's hands. Whatever they had in mind now, Ross was right. The pain searing through her ankle would seem as blissful as the aromatherapy massage she'd enjoyed at the Malmaison. She shivered.

"We can't outrun them," Ross said. "We've got to find a hiding place."

"There," Amy pointed to the right hand fork.

Like a beacon, a grey metal door was inset into the wall a mere twenty metres away. Kat detached herself from Amy and ran to it. "It's open," she reported.

They heard footsteps at a running pace.

"It's our only chance," Ross said. Half-carrying Amy, he dragged her to the door.

They'd found a small chamber, roughly square, empty save for a few boxes. "We need to lock ourselves in," Ross said, "or make a barricade, or even set an ambush."

Amy put her finger to her lips. They all heard Shaun's voice, loud, clear and near, as Amy gently pushed the door fully shut.

Chapter 38 Shaun

"That's enough," Shaun said sharply, wrinkling his nose at the acrid smell of the burning shrub. "No fires here, not until I've seen the whites of her eyes. I want my money back."

He turned his attention to the black door in front of them. It was firmly shut. Frustrated, Shaun pushed against it to see how solid it was. Clearly, the wood and hinges were strong; there was no movement. He considered asking Jeb to batter it, and discounted the possibility. It would be noisy, without any guarantee of success. Instead, Shaun inspected the lock. He had a couple of bump keys he kept for situations like this, but no hammer or screwdriver with which to tap them. Swiftly, he removed a lock-picking tool from his wallet. Shaun's father had taught him well; he and Jeb were inside the property within thirty seconds.

"Cover me, Jeb," he said, kicking open the door on the left. In truth, he was sure Marty Bridges was not there. They would be facing Kat, Ross and perhaps Amy; no one else. In any event, Jeb steadied his gun as Shaun glanced around the empty room. "We'll try the door on the right next," he said.

"Okay." Jeb's consonants were muffled, probably because his nose was broken. Shaun had little sympathy. He regretted praising Jeb so quickly. Erik's corpse was an inconvenience they could do without.

Opening the right hand door revealed the steps to the cellar. "The light's on. Let's get down there." He removed his pistol from his breast pocket and held it in front of him, ready to shoot. "Have your gun ready too, Jeb. No need to worry about the sound. These walls are solid." He hoped the floors weren't. A bare earth cellar was a useful place to dispose of bodies; Erik's, for example. They could drag it there later when they'd despatched the fugitives.

"Okay," Jeb, usually more talkative, muttered again.

The stairs twisted to the left through ninety degrees and opened out into a brick vault. Shaun's pleasure at spying the dirt floor turned swiftly to dismay. Apart from broken old furniture and other bric-a-brac, the gloomy underground room was empty. "Where are they?" he said, outraged.

"In the shade?" Jeb asked, shooting liberally at the larger shadows.

"Stop that," Shaun said sharply, as a couple of bullets ricocheted in random directions, almost returning to sender.

"Since when were you a poster boy for health and safety?" Jeb whinged.

"Is there another way out?" Shaun mused. "I can't see any doors. Got a light, Jeb?"

Jeb's cigarette lighter flared, adding enough illumination to discern dusty footprints heading towards the back of the room.

"That's it," Shaun said. "There's a door behind those shelves. Pull everything off them."

Jeb roughly cleared the upper shelves of the rusty unit, sending old boxes and metal coils thudding to the ground. He dragged the unit to one side.

Shaun tutted impatiently. Luckily, the door wasn't locked. Shaun opened it to reveal the spiral ladder beyond. He heard a distant clang as a door slammed shut far below. While he could barely see, he knew he was on Kat's trail. "This is it," he breathed. "There must be another cellar down there. We'll catch them like rats in a trap. Do you have anything better than that cigarette lighter?"

"I left the flamethrower at home," Jeb joked.

Shaun gave him a filthy look, completely wasted in the gloom, he knew. "Okay, we'll just have to be careful," he said. "Put your gun away. You go first, with your lighter."

"One of my phones has a flashlight," Jeb said. Like Shaun, he always carried a few; cheap models on pay as you go tariffs, completely untraceable.

"Mine too," Shaun admitted. "Sorted." He ordered Jeb to descend first, carrying the light. He, Shaun, would follow with his gun, to provide cover.

The substantial metal door at the foot was a problem. They tried pushing and pulling, but it remained firmly locked. Furthermore, it appeared to be built to withstand an earthquake. Even Jeb couldn't lever it off its hinges, bruising his shoulder when he tried.

"We'll just have to guess at the combination," Shaun said. "I wish my boys were here. It's like a password, isn't it?" He recalled Ben saying most passwords were common, and therefore easy to hack.

"One," Jeb suggested.

"It won't be a single number," Shaun said, twisting the dial to one, releasing it and repeating the process twice. The door stayed stubbornly shut. He searched the corners of his mind for inspiration, apprehensively trying one, two, three. "Bingo." The metal door opened.

"It's the Tube," Jeb exclaimed. "All aboard the Piccadilly Line."

They were at the blind end of a tunnel, constructed of white painted bricks and running for about fifty metres before emerging in a T junction. At the top of the curved ceiling was a strip of fluorescent lights accompanied by thick worms of cable. Shaun wondered what this place was, and its purpose. Knowing he was below Birmingham's Jewellery Quarter, it occurred to him that the underground passages might give him access for a jewel heist in future. Marty Bridges' disused workshop was both an excellent entry point and escape route. It was a stroke of luck, not only that Kat had been hiding there, but that Jeb had not yet put the workshop on fire as Shaun had intended.

Shaun resolved to explore the subterranean warren once he'd given Kat what she deserved. He agreed it resembled the London Underground, although no tracks were laid on the smooth concrete floor. There were none of the sights, sounds and smells of the Tube, either. Most striking of all, he and Jeb were alone. There was no sign of Kat and her friends. "Sshh," he cautioned. "Listen for them."

They stood still and silent. At first, all Shaun heard was a low hum of machinery and another sound, barely audible, like a bath filling. Then a woman spoke, her comments indistinct. Shaun pointed to the left of the T junction, looking at Jeb. Jeb nodded. They ran.

At the T junction, another tunnel, similar to the first except for its length, curved away in both directions. Shaun and Jeb sprinted to the left. Round the bend, there was a long, straight stretch, then a fork. No voices were audible.

Shaun's mind was racing. Which direction should they choose? He simply didn't know. "We'll split up," he decided. "Get your gun ready again."

"You want me to make a public announcement, boss?" Jeb asked, with the merest hint of insolence, albeit obeying swiftly.

Shaun glared. "They'll know we're coming. We sound like a herd of elephants already." Indeed, there was no way of muffling their footsteps on the hard floor. "Whoever sees them first – shout, okay?"

Jeb grunted assent.

Shaun took the right hand fork. He was still fit enough to run fast. It was a skill, the only one in fact, that had won him prizes at school and it had saved him in his teens when burglaries went wrong. As always, he kept his senses in a state of high alert. That was how he noticed a ringing noise from a door on his left, as if it had been abruptly closed and an echo remained.

It was a grey metal door, smaller and plainer than the entrance to the underground complex. Shaun pushed it cautiously. It opened a crack. While there was light beyond, he could see nothing else. He applied more force, and the door swung wide open.

This was a room, a cuboid; painted white like the thoroughfares around him but devoid of curves. Its function was unclear. Perhaps it was a little-used storeroom, for a few cardboard boxes were scattered around. Of more interest, Kat and her two friends were also there, shrinking in a corner.

There was no hiding place in the almost-empty chamber, no doors through which they could escape. He had them in his sights at last.

"I've got a gun," he said, pointing it at Kat, "and I'm not afraid to use it."

"I didn't think it was a vase of flowers, Shaun," she said.

He wanted to laugh, but stopped himself. If she hadn't been so greedy, he might have bought her flowers; a lavish bouquet redolent of his wealth and power. There was no point speculating about a fantasy Kat, though. He'd misjudged the real Kat, failed to understand what she was prepared to do for money. Twenty grand was twenty grand. "Jeb!" he shouted. He could have despatched them all in seconds, but he wanted his henchman to see the act, to tell others and have it pass into folklore. He couldn't afford his peers to think he was a soft touch. "Don't move," he snarled at the trio.

They huddled in the furthest corner of the room, a mere few yards from him. Shaun had imagined the young, besuited man he'd punched in the courtyard was Amy's boyfriend. They'd been together at the pub in Harborne. No longer; the young man was holding Kat's hand, an impassive expression on his bespectacled face. While Amy leaned against the wall, fidgeting and anxious, Kat was cool and poised as ever. Shaun admired her nerve.

Jeb arrived, waving a pistol flamboyantly. "You found them, boss?" His eyes were a mixture of triumph and fear. What was that about?

"Put that away, Jeb," Shaun ordered.

Jeb moved his gun, almost imperceptibly, as if steadying it. Within a split-second, Shaun saw Amy push Kat away from the corner, simultaneously hearing the crack of a bullet leaving Jeb's pistol. Amy grimaced, apparently in pain. The bullet hadn't touched her, though. Shaun saw it hit the wall, bouncing harmlessly into one of the cardboard boxes.

Shaun had no chance to speak. Kat's male friend, who like Kat had been caught off-balance and ended up on the ground, dived forward

178

and rugby tackled Jeb's ankles. His black-rimmed spectacles fell and shattered.

Jeb fell on top of the man, landing a punch on him but dropping his gun. Shaun kicked it behind him before his captives could consider any further heroics. "Nobody move," he ordered. He turned his attention to his henchman. "I'm doing the shooting, okay? Just me and nobody else."

"I'd get on with it if I were you, boss," Jeb said. "We don't know who else is around."

"Have you heard anyone?"

Jeb strained his ears, before shaking his head. "No, boss."

"Good." Satisfied they all knew who called the shots, Shaun approached Kat. She was wearing a long silk kimono, a garment that revealed little skin, but every inch of her curves. He reached to stroke her hair, noting with amusement how the young man glared. How much could he see without his spectacles? Shaun wasn't taking any chances. He pointed his gun at the man.

Kat herself didn't flinch. Her gorgeous green eyes caught his. "Why do you want to kill me, Shaun?" she asked.

"You took the money, Kat," Shaun said, almost sorrowfully.

The young man couldn't contain himself. "How much is it?" he asked contemptuously. "I'll write you a cheque."

Shaun was implacable. "No cheques. My business is cash only. And it's too late. Nobody crosses me. They don't steal from me. Nobody, do you hear me? At least, not if they want to live." His raised voice echoed in the brick chamber.

He could have insisted on a trip to the cash machine, he supposed, but what was the point of that? At most, the lad could have withdrawn five hundred pounds, while Shaun would run the risk of betrayal, not to mention walking past a bevy of CCTV cameras.

Kat looked into Shaun's eyes again. "I didn't steal anything," she said.

"No," Jeb interjected angrily.

179

"Let her finish," Shaun told him. "Twenty grand disappeared from the backroom at AKD," he said to Kat.

"Where was it – just lying around? I never saw money in there," Kat said, seemingly puzzled. "Did you, Jeb? He's talking about the room where you gave me a thousand pounds and told me to lie low."

Shaun looked at Jeb, realising at once why his subordinate's eyes shifted away from his.

"Vince," Jeb said, his voice dripping with sincerity. "Honest to God, it must have been."

Shaun hid his shock at the treachery behind an icy mask. "I know what I need to know," he said.

He knew he was a good marksman too. The bullet pierced Jeb's heart in an instant.

Chapter 39 Amy

Amy screamed.

Nothing happened. The US cavalry, her fairy godmother, even the West Midlands Police – all were conspicuous by their absence. As if frozen in time, Shaun still stood before her with a gun in his hand. Jeb lay on the concrete floor, a red stain growing like a flower on his white T-shirt. Kat's mouth was open, but no sound emerged; she was clutching Ross' arm for comfort.

"Shut up. You're giving me a headache," Shaun said savagely.

Amy willed herself into silence, staring at him in fear and disbelief. She might as well have shot Kat and Ross herself. If it hadn't been for her arrival at Erik's flat, Jeb and Shaun would never have known where Kat was, wouldn't have stayed to see Ross return from London. She shivered. Shaun would never let them go. He could not.

As if echoing her thoughts, Shaun said, with a trace of regret in his tone, "It wasn't you, then, sweetheart. I came all this way for nothing. It's a shame you had to see this, but that's too bad." He sighed.

"Let us go," Ross pleaded. "You know Kat's done nothing to harm you. None of us have."

Shaun frowned. "Like I said, it's too bad."

"Kill me, not her," Ross said.

Shaun sneered. "You're dying anyway. Do you think I want witnesses?" He steadied his gun.

Ross dived again. He threw himself forward, reaching for Shaun's ankles and curling himself up to deliver a blow from his skull to Shaun's groin as the bigger man fell down. The gun was fired uselessly in the air.

Amy noticed Kat gawping at Ross, admiration plain on her face. Who knew how long that would last? If they couldn't escape, he'd never profit from it.

Ross grappled with Shaun for the gun. It was clear that Shaun wasn't relinquishing it easily. He pulled the trigger whenever he could, spraying the room with slugs at random. They ricocheted in different directions. Mere chance saved them from a hit.

Ross' luck ran out. A bullet clipped his knee. He screamed in agony, momentarily giving Shaun the upper hand.

It wasn't the only gun in the room, of course. Amy saw the same realisation dawn on Kat's face as she eyed Jeb's dead body. While Kat swooped down on Jeb's weapon, Amy hobbled towards Shaun.

The gangster was preoccupied by his fight. Gritting her teeth, her ankle throbbing, Amy stamped on Shaun's right arm. Indescribable pain exploded in her foot, but it was worth it. At last, Shaun let go of his gun. She kicked it away before falling to her knees, sobbing.

"Freeze," Kat said, and then louder, "I've got a gun and I know how to use it."

The effect was electric. Shaun and Ross ceased struggling and gawped at her.

"Put that down," Shaun said finally. "A girl like you shouldn't go near a dangerous weapon like that."

"Don't call my bluff," Kat said.

Shaun made no further protest.

"Tie him up," Kat commanded.

"We're rather short of rope, Kat. I'll use my tie." Ross stared at her, wide-eyed.

Despite the pain seething through her, Amy had to suppress a grin. Ross wasn't used to being given orders, except by the redoubtable Cari. Nevertheless, he did as he was told.

It was a typical city tie, co-ordinated precisely with his shirt and cufflinks, and had probably cost more than Amy spent on a week's food. Ross unknotted the delicate silk length and roughly bound Shaun's hands behind his back. He wasn't gentle.

"Nothing for the legs, sorry," Ross said. "Anyway, we can't carry him all the way back to the surface. Like this, he'll climb the ladder, and we'll hand him in to the police."

"Who says we're telling the police?" Kat replied.

Chapter 40 Shaun

Shaun woke drenched in sweat. No light emerged through the bars at his window, apart from the feeble orange glow that clung to cities late at night. No birds sang.

His nightmare still gripped his heart, Meg's words echoing in his mind. "You killed the man who would have cured me."

Shaun shook his head. "He isn't dead," he whispered.

Not only that, but Meg had said no such thing, had never had reason to do so in the real world from which she'd departed three years before. The ache of seeing her again, even in the shifting landscape of a dream, brought tears to his eyes. A quite unfamiliar emotion, guilt, enveloped him.

That was exactly what Kat wanted to achieve, he reflected bitterly. As soon as the police told her that her brother had been found with his throat cut, she'd rounded on Shaun. Icily, she'd informed him her brother was developing a cure for cancer. His wife, Kat said, would turn in her grave.

The police had arrived in the nick of time; the first occasion in his life when he'd been pleased to see the Old Bill. Kat would have put a bullet in his brain for sure, or left him to starve, even before she knew about her brother. Her eyes, like cold, hard chips of jade, haunted him as he drifted back to sleep.

Morning came. He paced his cell, remembering the sheer boredom of prison, contemplating his future with dread. Even if his brief could reduce the charges, Shaun was bound to serve a long stretch. Right now, he'd been arrested on one count of murder and two attempted murders, the latter still a surprise to him as he'd imagined Jeb would actually manage to kill someone when he put his mind to it.

Poverty awaited beyond the prison sentence. His business activities were on the wrong side of the law, and it wouldn't take long to establish that. Everything he owned – the house in Wanstead, the casino, nail bars, property and car – all would be seized by the government. It was their revenge for the taxes he'd never paid, he supposed.

He would have to break it to the boys. Finally, they'd have to earn a living, by fair means or foul.

"You've never seen me in a place like this," Shaun said, when they visited. "I haven't been inside for nearly thirty years. Not nice, is it?"

Ben pushed his floppy blond fringe back from his brown eyes. They were wide as saucers. He nodded.

Jon, the younger one, stared at the bars. "Seen worse on TV," he muttered.

"I'm too old for this lark," Shaun sighed. "Prison's for younger men." He could handle it, though: the poor diet, pointless work, enforced idleness and tedium. There would be business to do inside and he'd acquire useful connections. His crimes, and certainly his fists, commanded respect.

Ben shrugged.

"You'll both need to work," Shaun began to say.

"Gaming," Ben said.

"That's your hobby," Shaun said, speaking slowly, as if to an idiot. "I mean, you'll have to earn money."

"I will, at the gaming tournament. I'm in line for twenty grand prize money, representing north London," Ben said, to Shaun's astonishment.

"A prize for playing computer games?"

"Yes, at Excel, next week. It's the national tournament, right? Thousands of people pay to watch. I'm favourite to win it."

"You?" Shaun was shaken at the news. It was as if his son had a secret life. He found himself gripped with pride. "Where can I place a bet on that?"

"I've got that sorted," Jon said.

"Jon's running a book online," Ben said dismissively. "On the dark net."

185

"What's that? Is it legal?" Shaun asked.

"Well, duh," Jon replied. "Anyway, what about your criminal empire – who's going to lead that for you? The drugs, the fencing, the casino?"

"How do you know about those?" Shaun asked. He'd never said a great deal about his work to his sons, at least not once they'd made it clear they had no interest in doing any.

"It was all over primary school," Jon said, rolling his eyes.

"Did it get you into fights?" Shaun asked, remembering occasions in his childhood when he'd desperately wished his father wasn't in and out of prison.

"None I couldn't win," Jon said contemptuously.

Shaun studied his younger son. He was taller than Ben, dark haired, his face a jumble of angles. Shaun had looked the same at that age, until his features settled into a more pleasing picture.

"Let me run the business while you're away," Jon said. "Just tell me how to get started – and who I can trust."

"If there's one thing we've learned in gaming, it's that you need to know who your friends are," Ben said.

"Strategy's important too," his brother added.

There was hope then, a chance they'd succeed. Shaun hardly knew his children, yet they were his own flesh and blood. Somewhere, beneath those idle facades, lay the genes for a thriving criminal enterprise. His brain went into overdrive, as he tried to distil a lifetime's knowledge and experience into thirty minutes.

"The casino's sorted," Shaun said. "Vince will take care of it. You know Vince, don't you?"

Ben and Jon both nodded. Vince had been a frequent guest at barbeques and other family parties, in the days when Meg was around to organise them.

"You can trust him," Shaun said. "Up to a point, anyway. If you think he's ripping you off, send word to me." His nostrils flared. "I can make trouble for him – when I get out, definitely. Almost certainly before then, as well. People know I've killed a man who crossed me. That counts in this world."

Jon nodded. "What about the rest?"

"Keep up the bootlegging. The team may think about going freelance. Offer them a bigger cut to keep them sweet. Don't bother with the drugs, girls and stolen goods. Too risky. Great money, but also a great chance of being grassed on or taking a knife in your back. If I was starting over, I wouldn't touch them, knowing what I know now. And set up a couple of nail bars and hair salons. A tanning centre. Hot dog stands where the students hang out. Cash businesses, that's what you want. Maybe a laundromat. You can literally wash your money clean." He shrugged. "You'll pay a bit of tax, but it's worth it, because you'll keep what's left."

Shaun fidgeted. He had to impart an uncomfortable truth. "Life is going to change," he said. "My brief says everything I own will be taken away by the law. You need to look after yourselves. Take what you can and run, if you need to. And especially, if someone makes you an offer for the casino, a good offer, take it and run off to Spain."

He ought to tell them about the money too. He doubted they'd squander it. They rarely smoked, drank or touched drugs as far as he could tell. Video games left no time for anything else. "There's fifty grand in used notes up in the loft," he said. "It'll keep the two of you going for a year or so if you're careful, so don't spend it all at once. And don't leave it somewhere obvious, where the Old Bill will find it, or an idiot with a death wish coming round to rob you. Only fools stick cash under mattresses. There's a machete under mine for emergencies; nothing else. Put one under yours too. The loft's a good bet for concealing valuables. Nobody ever looks there." He knew all the common hiding places and had burgled most of them in his time.

"Thanks," Ben said. He patted Shaun's shoulder. "We'll visit you, Dad."

Chapter 41 Amy

Seeing Erik in hospital meant taking a taxi, past Florence Street and then swiftly away from the industrial core of the city through the green-leaved suburbs beyond. While there was plenty of room for three people, the cab seemed claustrophobic. Amy glanced at Ross, his arm around Kat's shoulder. Remembering their night together at the Malmaison, she felt uncomfortable. She occupied herself by staring out of the window.

Like much of Birmingham, the hospital was new: a sleek, curved statement of a building, squatting like an alien spaceship in the red brick suburbs. Ross had only just been discharged from A&E himself and was still hobbling with the aid of a crutch. Despite this, he immediately took charge, asking for Erik at the reception desk and then leading the girls to the ward.

Kat's brother already had a visitor. A middle-aged woman sat on a plastic chair next to his bed, sharing liquorice allsorts and flicking through the pages of a James Patterson novel with him. Erik himself was propped up on pillows, a bandage around his neck and a morphine drip attached to his arm. His face was mottled with bruises.

On first sight, Amy imagined his companion was Lizzie. About to offer congratulations at the cleaner's speedy recovery, she suddenly realised this was a stranger: younger than Lizzie and shorter, blonde bobbed hair streaked auburn and a mischievous grin on her face.

"Hello, I'm Jackie," Erik's guest said. Like Lizzie, she was clearly local. "You must be this young man's friends. He's been through the wars, hasn't he?"

"That he has," Ross agreed. To his credit, he said nothing about his own injuries: the painful knee, and the bruises.

Kat kissed Erik's cheeks. "I'm so glad you're okay," she said, handing him a huge box of Belgian chocolates. Ross had hastily bought them at Amy's suggestion.

"We're all glad," Ross emphasised. In Kat's company, he was charm personified.

"I owe my life to this lady here," Erik said, beaming at Jackie.

Jackie blushed. "I did what anyone would do," she said.

"What happened?" Amy asked, although she already knew the bare facts. Jeb had cut Erik's throat and left him for dead. It was a miracle that Kat's brother could be sitting here, smiling and chatting with them.

"I don't remember much," Erik said. "There were two of them. I suppose you know that?"

Amy nodded.

"I thought so," Erik said ruefully. "I was fighting both men. I gave the younger one a bloody nose, then wrestled with his mate. He might have been past his prime, but he was strong. The black eyes came from him." He pointed. "It was the young guy, Jeb, who did the real damage, though. He had a knife, or maybe a razor." Erik drew a finger across his neck. "He cut me above the Adam's apple. Had he slashed me below it, across the carotid artery, I would be dead. He certainly thought I was. They both did. I was bleeding heavily, after all."

Amy saw Kat's eyes glisten.

"They left me alone, then," Erik said. "They were only interested in chasing you. My priority was to stem the bleeding. I staggered back into the flat, found a cushion and thrust it against my neck. Then I went outside."

"You didn't phone the police?" Ross asked.

"No. I could barely speak or breathe. The trauma and blood loss drained my energy. I knew I wouldn't get far. But if I'd stayed in the workshop or courtyard, no one would have found me. Somehow, I staggered to the road…"

"…and then I came along," Jackie said. "I can't pretend it wasn't a shock to see you, white as a sheet, blood everywhere."

"I bumped into her," Erik said. "Why don't you tell them about it, Jackie?"

189

"All that blood made a mess of my new summer dress," Jackie deadpanned. "Seriously."

"Actually," Erik said, "Jackie called for an ambulance. She wrapped me in a coat. Although it was a warm day, I was beginning to shiver and lose consciousness. She kept me talking so I'd stay awake."

"I seem to recall I did the talking," Jackie said.

Erik laughed. "True enough, as I was in no state to chat. I couldn't have imagined what topics to discuss with a stab victim, but Jackie made a valiant attempt. We talked about music, TV and the best place for a cocktail in Birmingham. And her work. Jackie's a librarian, so I have a long list of books to read now."

"You were lucky I'd finished work early that day," Jackie said. "I was on my way to meet a friend at the Pen Museum."

"Is that another cocktail bar?" Ross asked.

Amy was about to say she doubted it. She was sure it was simply a quirky museum; she'd seen signs for it on her walk through the Jewellery Quarter. Neither she nor Jackie had a chance to reply, though, for Kat turned to the librarian. "Where do you recommend for a cocktail?"

"The Jekyll & Hyde. They make possibly the meanest Long Island Iced Tea in the known universe. Certainly the finest in the city. "

"Want to try it later?" Amy asked Kat.

Kat's eyes sparkled. "Perhaps after I've shown Ross the sights."

"Don't you need to be getting back to London, Amy?" Ross asked. "You'll need a sick note if you stay away from work any longer. I'll take Kat to sample the Long Island Iced Tea for you."

"It's the weekend now," Amy pointed out, while realising the last thing she wanted was to spend more time with Ross. She glared sourly at him as he clutched Kat's hand like a lovesick adolescent. Erik caught her eye. He flashed a sympathetic glance. Clearly, he'd divined the tension between the two colleagues. She hoped he couldn't guess the reason.

"What I want to know," Erik said, "is what happened in the cellar. The police say one of the men who attacked me is in prison, and the other dead."

"Yes," Amy said. "The man who cut your throat, Jeb, was shot by his friend."

"Ross and Amy saved my life in that tunnel," Kat said.

"And you saved ours," Ross said loyally. "She picked up Jeb's gun and told Shaun she would use it."

"I have no doubt she would have done." A smile illuminated Erik's face.

"Somehow, the police knew we were there," Amy said. "They turned up in force, once Jeb was dead and we'd overpowered Shaun."

"I asked Jackie to phone them," Erik admitted.

Kat breathed in sharply.

"What else should I have done?" Erik said. "I knew what those men were capable of. You obviously didn't. You regarded them as your friends, even." He shook his head. "I called the police to protect you."

"They would have come anyway," Jackie said. "When a man's throat is slashed, you know it wasn't a household accident. And did I hear you were wandering around the Anchor tunnels? In that case, someone, somewhere was watching you, I bet. Those tunnels hold too many secrets. Nobody's supposed to have access. You can be sure the police were on their way already."

"Kat, you really mustn't worry," Ross said. "Ted's confident he can resolve any difficulties with the police."

He might have to arrange a divorce too, Amy thought, recalling Lulu's cautionary words. Kat and Ahmed were man and wife in the eyes of the law, assuming it wasn't a bigamous marriage. There was good reason to suspect it was, though, because the police had mentioned Bronwen's name too. How many identities had Kat stolen at Jeb's prompting? She'd be legally married to her first groom. Amy shuddered, relieved, as Lulu had said, it wasn't her problem.

191

"You won't go back to London now, will you Kat?" Erik asked anxiously.

"I'll stay here until you're better," she promised.

"And I'll be here with you," Ross said.

"You'll visit Lizzie too, I guess," Erik suggested. "She's still in hospital and in quite a state, I hear."

"You can rely on me," Kat said.

"Good." Erik smiled.

Amy found his happy mood was infectious. When Erik's eyes twinkled, he was a different person, a far more likable one than the man scrabbling through boxes in Kat's room. He'd been so focused on retrieving his possessions that he had no time for social niceties, she supposed.

Jackie looked at her watch. "Actually, I have to be going. My husband's taking me to a rock concert. I hope you like the book. It's a popular one." She pointed to the novel.

"Wait," Erik said. "Can I buy you a drink next week? I expect I'll be out of here, and I'd like to treat you, to say thanks. Anyway, I need to give your book back. What was that place you recommended – the Jekyll & Hyde?"

"Yes, or the champagne bar in the Mailbox. Half-price on Fridays."

"I'll see you there next Friday evening."

She winked at him as she left.

Kat began to laugh. "I've been so worried about you," she said. "You've been completely obsessed with darria for so long. Now, at last, you have a date!"

"Not in a romantic sense," Erik protested. "It's just a gesture of thanks. Jackie's older than me, and more to the point, she's happily married."

"Who's Darria?" Ross asked.

Kat raised an eyebrow. "It's a boring little bush, a mean, shrubby thing. Erik thinks he can cure cancer with it."

192

"I don't think, I know," Erik protested. "My research proves it. Darria can save millions of lives."

"So why isn't it on every pharmacy's shelves already?" Kat scoffed. "I'll tell you why, Erik. It's because you're chasing an impossible dream. Far better to go back home and negotiate with the authorities to get the Snow Mountain factory back. We have a strong legal case and they know it."

Ross gaped at her. "What do you mean?" he asked.

"You'll help me, won't you, Ross? You've got contacts. Erik and I are rightful owners of the Snow Mountain vodka brand. Erik's so-called friend and landlord, Marty Bridges, sold us down the river." Kat turned to her brother. "I don't know how that snake can look you in the eye," she spat.

"Of course I'll help you, Kat," Ross said.

"Hey, what's this? A family gathering?"

Amy looked up. Marty Bridges was striding into the ward, a big grin on his face and a bottle of vodka in his hand. A young nurse was trailing after him, her expression worried.

"No alcohol here," she said to him.

He thrust the bottle in her hand. "No worries, bab," he said. "Here, you take this as a little gift for looking after my business partner so well."

"Business partner?" Kat said. "What's going on?" She looked horrified.

"That's right," Marty declared. "Erik and I will be selling darria tea to cure the Big C."

"Not exactly," Erik said. "We'll be researching and commercialising a darria-based medicine."

"Indeed," Marty agreed. "It'll cost me an arm and a leg. So I'm afraid I can't invest in your insurance start-up after all, Ross, attractive though it is."

"How dare you," Kat said.

Marty shrugged. "I'm sorry, bab. I just don't have enough money."

193

"No." Kat's cheeks flushed. She rounded on Erik. "You can't do this. You're betraying our parents' memory."

"I need investment to take my research further," Erik said. "Besides, you've judged Marty too harshly. He's helped us both. You wouldn't have your precious British passport without him."

Would it have been better if she hadn't? Amy mused. Without it, Kat would have presented a less alluring prospect to Jeb. He might never have suggested she marry visa over-stayers if she hadn't possessed a British passport in the first place.

"He does nothing unless there's something in it for him," Kat responded. She must hate Marty with a passion. "Do you think he'd give you the time of day if he couldn't make big bucks from your darria drug?"

"That's capitalism, dear," Ross said, squeezing her hand and winking at Marty.

"You're all crazy," Kat flared, pulling away from him and stomping out of the ward.

Ross followed her as Marty looked on in amusement.

"Sorry to break up the party," Marty grinned.

"She'll get over it," Erik said. "Ross will calm her down."

Amy didn't doubt it. Kat had offered to show Ross round the city. Amy suspected that meant the designer boutiques of the Mailbox, the chic shopping centre wrapped around the Malmaison. The tempting artisan shops of the Jewellery Quarter would probably make the list too. Amy sighed. Kat was a high maintenance woman, but at least with Ross' deep pockets at her disposal, she needn't marry the likes of Ahmed again.

"Amy, stop here for a few minutes. There's something I want to ask you," Marty said. "Erik, you'll never guess. I've been talking to young Parveen – you know, my neighbour's daughter."

"I may have met her many years ago," Erik said. "What of it?"

"She speaks very highly of young Amy here. They've been working together in marketing."

194

Amy stared at Marty in dismay. Whatever his intentions, it would be obvious to Parveen now that Amy's sick leave wasn't genuine. Monday morning seemed even less appealing than usual.

"We need a marketing specialist," Erik said.

"Exactly," Marty said. "What do you think, bab? How about working for us?"

Chapter 42 Marty

Marty had made the job offer flippantly. He was pleasantly surprised by Erik's reaction.

"I'd love you to work with us, Amy," Kat's brother said, "as long as you understand one thing." He had his serious air again. "You must realise that commercialising the cancer cure is an all-consuming passion for me. It's what my life's all about. I'll work hard, and often I'll expect you to work hard too, because nothing else matters."

Amy looked stunned. Marty felt a pang of sympathy for her. She was clearly still processing the suggestion. "You don't have to decide now," he said gently. "I have my own ideas about business strategy and marketing. Phone me on Monday and we can discuss them. Erik looks tired. I'll give you a lift back to your hotel."

"See you again soon," Erik said. His intense green eyes were locked onto Amy's. He offered her his right hand, pulling her towards him when she took it and kissing her cheek.

"Take care," Amy said weakly.

Marty jingled his car keys, glad that Amy took the hint and followed him. "You could do a lot worse," he said, when they were out of Erik's earshot.

"What do you mean?"

"I saw the way Erik looked at you. He's as good as gold, you know, worth twenty of Mr Smooth Bastard Ross Pritchard."

She winced.

"I obviously got that wrong," Marty said.

"No, I've twisted my ankle," Amy replied.

"You too? I noticed Pritchard was limping. What have you been doing?" Marty teased. "Wait at the door and I'll bring the car."

He saluted her like a chauffeur once he'd collected his sleek silver Jaguar. "You and Ross aren't returning to London in that condition, are you?" he asked.

"I will," Amy said. "Not Ross."

"Very wise," Marty chuckled. "Leave the lovebirds together. You know the story of Icarus who flew too close to the sun?"

"Remind me."

"It's a Greek legend." Marty read extensively when he flew around the globe on business. "Icarus had a pair of wings. He was warned that the sun's heat would destroy them, but he flew near it anyway. The warnings came true. I see Kat as the hot sun. Like Icarus, people are attracted to her, but they ought to be careful." Marty gestured around him. "Erik knows that. That's why he lives here, a hundred miles away from his sister."

"He'll move to London, though, won't he? To set up his business."

"That's not how it works, bab," Marty said cheerfully. "He's managed perfectly well in Brum until now, especially as I only charge him a pittance in rent. I like it here too, for that matter."

"The marketing job is in Birmingham, then?"

"Oh yes," Marty said. "Parveen will be peeved, but so what? She can't expect everyone in her team to stick to her like a shadow." He added, "I think you'll like it here. In London, everyone wears a mask, pretending to be a brighter, shinier version of themselves. I don't see that in you and you won't find me pretending to be anyone I'm not. What you see is what you get. Erik's the same."

Amy nodded, lips pursed, apparently unimpressed.

"I'm not always politically correct," Marty admitted. He dimly recalled making a statement about feminine logic when they last met. Perhaps that had annoyed her. "Let's talk on Monday. You owe it to Erik, at least."

Chapter 43 Amy

The Malmaison allowed Amy to check out late. She presumed Ross had already arranged it with them. Her first class rail return in her pocket, her bag neatly packed and her emotions rather less organised, she took a cab to New Street station. It annoyed her that she was unable to walk such a short distance. An unexpected sense of loss assailed her as the train began its journey away from the city.

She had to take a taxi from Euston too. Arriving home, Amy opened her front door apprehensively. Luckily, the flat was just as she'd left it. Checking Kat's room just to make sure, she uncovered no evidence of further dubious callers. At last, a Sunday morning lie-in beckoned. Dreams called to Amy even before her head hit the pillow.

Sunday dawned bright and clear, according to the BBC weather forecast at any rate. Amy's windows on the outside world were small, at the top of one of her bedrooms walls, and perpetually in shade. Only the heat within the room gave a hint of the elements outside.

For breakfast, she would have to limp to Pret, if not to a supermarket. The store cupboard had yielded only mouldy bread; the fridge, sour milk. Unlocking the front door, she was unprepared for the smart, loafer-shod foot that immediately planted itself inside the hallway.

Amy gasped, looking up into the craggy face of the large gentleman to whom the foot belonged. In his thirties, with the twisted nose and ears of a rugby player or boxer, he appeared ill at ease in his suit. "Good morning, Madam," he said conversationally. "May we come in?"

She noticed the equally sturdy, somewhat more polished, besuited fellow behind him. "Certainly not," she said. Deciding they were probably Jehovah's Witnesses, she resolved to be polite. "If you have a leaflet about your church meetings, please leave it with me."

"No church leaflets," said the second man, not quite succeeding in suppressing a grin. "We're bailiffs appointed by the owner to take possession of this flat." He showed her a plastic identity card. "Here's my certificate, darling."

"The landlord has a county court possession order, Madam," his companion said. "Are you Miss Katharine White?"

"No, I'm her friend." Amy's head began to spin. "You'd better come in," she said. "I can't offer you tea, though, unless you take it black."

"No problem, darling."

She took them to Kat's room, to the sofa and folding chairs. Her rent, of course, had been paid to Kat regularly. That signified nothing, however. It was Kat's responsibility to pay the landlord, and it appeared Kat had not done so.

"What are the arrears?" she asked.

"Five months."

Although Kat had collected rent, then, she hadn't paid any during the whole of Amy's residence at the property, and much of Bronwen's. How, Amy wondered, could she raise funds to clear the arrears? Charles was unlikely to help. Ross might, though. "I'll just make a phone call to get the cash for you," she said.

The rugby player frowned. "It's too late, Madam. We're here to evict you. I must ask you to allow us to inspect this flat, and seize such assets as we see fit to make good the arrears. All other goods will be placed outside and you must remove them from the premises."

"We'll change the locks," his companion said.

"You shouldn't take my things," Amy said. "I don't owe any rent."

They agreed this was reasonable, as she wasn't Miss Katharine White. In the event, they took bags full of designer clothes and shoes from Kat's room. The girls' other belongings were placed neatly in the car park, where Amy sat on a wine crate and watched as the locks were changed.

199

Chapter 44 Ross

Ross had enjoyed a most satisfactory night, and wasn't best pleased to take a call from Amy on Sunday morning.

"They did what?" he said stiffly. "For crying out loud, how could you let that happen?" He'd never been visited by bailiffs – there was no reason why a man of his means should ever meet one – but he knew that, like vampires, they could only cross the threshold if invited.

"What's the matter?" Kat's green eyes were wide with alarm.

Ross softened. "Hold on," he said, muting the phone. "You've been evicted from your flat," he told Kat. "I'm sure it's a misunderstanding. You can move in with me."

She snuggled up to him. "And Amy?" she asked. "She has nowhere else to go."

"She can stay in my spare room, I suppose," Ross acceded with bad grace. "For a week or so, anyhow." If it was the price he must pay for Kat to live with him, it was worth it. Anyway, Amy could look after the flat while he was away with Kat in Birmingham and Thailand.

He spoke to Amy again. "Stay exactly where you are. I'm coming back to London. We'll move everything into my flat."

"I can't go with you," Kat said. "Erik is still in hospital."

"Don't worry," Ross replied, "I'll be back tonight."

He spent the bare minimum of time with Amy in London, both of them hobbling as they moved dresses, boxes and bags in and out of the lift and into his flat. Most of the items belonged to Kat. There was very little kitchen equipment, which suited Ross well as his designer kitchen was already well-stocked with sleek chrome gadgets. He gave Amy his spare keys, emphasised his expectations of tidiness, and departed for Euston to return to his new lover. His life was almost perfect. Only his minor leg wound and Amy's presence in his penthouse reminded Ross that his bliss was not a dream.

Although he thought nothing would stop him going to Thailand, fate intervened the following week.

Ted, his former schoolmate, arrived from London to represent Kat. "She's going to have to surrender her passport until her case is heard," Ted advised him over a pint.

Ross grimaced. "No holiday, then." He sent a brief email requesting a refund on his air tickets. While Ted's news was a blow, he was enjoying Kat's company in the slightly less exotic surroundings of Birmingham.

Minutes later, David Saxton phoned. "Do you think you could come back to work?" he asked. "Cari's been suspended. Of course, the rest of the actuarial team are covering, but I really need someone of your calibre around."

The call, while unexpected, was music to his ears. His presence must be vital to Veritable or Saxton wouldn't have phoned himself. Ross must make sure that Carolina Tait and Joanne Tonks found out, just to let them know where they stood in the pecking order. "Certainly, Davey," he said, with barely a thought for Snow Mountain. Anyhow, he didn't think Kat could do much to recover her family's vodka brand before her passport was returned. "You don't say no to David Saxton," he told Ted.

Chapter 45 Charles

Charles was at work, in the satisfying position of having delegated instructions to others to deal with the bank's latest IT crisis, when Davey Saxton rang.

"Let's have a drink after work," Davey said.

Charles knew better than to expect a blokey chinwag, but he wondered at Davey's agenda. It was a bit late to ask about Charles' intentions towards his sister.

Davey must have really wanted to meet him, because he agreed to see Charles at Canary Wharf. He insisted on a bar with good beer, which suited Charles fine.

"How's life at the bank?" Davey asked, when he'd bought their pints.

"Okay," Charles said.

"Are you getting a bonus for the investigation you did on us?"

"All in a day's work," Charles said. In truth, he suspected the incident had done more harm than good. Alex was even less inclined to trust him. "Look, Davey, I could do with a cigarette."

"We'll sit outside," Davey said.

Charles picked up his pint, even more puzzled. The tables outside were packed, but just starting to empty as drops of rain fell. They found a spot under a large umbrella. Charles lit a cigarette. "I suppose this is about Deirdre?" he asked.

Davey seemed surprised. "My sister's private life is none of my business."

Charles drew on his cigarette. The nicotine began to calm him. He decided to be straight with Davey. The man would find out soon anyway. "I assume you're aware," he said, "I'm moving out of Deirdre's place. I'm not saying we won't see each other, but I feel I got too serious too soon. I'm looking for a flat in Surrey Quays." It was time to step off the merry-go-round of parties, drinks, frequent holidays and wild sex, at least for a while. He needed time to breathe.

Davey caught his eye. "Are you sure about that?"

Charles prepared himself for an impassioned speech urging him to stay with Deirdre, but Davey merely said, "Be careful. In my experience, my sister usually gets what she wants." He looked around, obviously checking if anyone could overhear what he said to Charles, then dropped his voice to a whisper. "I suppose you've heard that Alana Green will be CEO of the merged company?"

"No," Charles said, truthfully. He hadn't heard, although it was the outcome Alex had predicted. Charles had been rather sceptical, given that Alana had been promoted to lead Bishopstoke less than a year before.

"There aren't too many female CEOs in the FTSE100 and she's young, black and American – she ticks a lot of boxes. The fund managers love her. Our generation is seen as pale, male and stale, I'm afraid."

Charles nodded. He was too aware of the contempt that Alex displayed for forty-somethings, seemingly ignorant that another decade would see him hit the big four-oh himself.

"However," Davey said, "There's life in this old dog yet. I've secured funding to set up a new insurance venture. It's very niche, dealing with certain risks for high net worth individuals. Kidnapping, business interruption, life insurance; that sort of thing. I'm taking young Ross with me. He's smart. What I want to know is, can I count you in as my IT Director? I can pay you twice what the bank does and you'll have an equity share as well."

"So you're offering me a job?"

"If you'll take it," Davey said. "You might want to think again about living in Surrey Quays. It's convenient enough for Canary Wharf, but I'll be taking office space in the City, in the Heron Tower." He laughed. "Poor Deirdre. She waited twenty five years for you. The

203

cool guy of the school. Captain of the football team. What I can't understand is why you went into IT?"

"I was good at it," Charles said. "And I wasn't going anywhere with the soccer. I sat on the waiting list for a trial with Charlton for a few years. I needed to be earning some money, especially marrying young, as I did."

"Charlton's loss is my gain, then," Davey said. "So you'll accept?"

Charles gathered he had some bargaining power. "The bank gives me a cheap mortgage," he said. "It's a stable career too. I could sit it out until retirement." As he said it, he realised he couldn't bear the thought. Working for Alex was already driving him to distraction. How much worse to do the same job year in, year out, as successive waves of young idiots like Alex were recruited to manage him.

In the end, they agreed that Charles would triple his salary. "Welcome on board," Davey said, clapping Charles' shoulder. "Another beer?"

Alex texted while Davey was at the bar. He wanted another early meeting next morning. Charles took great pleasure in replying that it was not convenient, and he would see Alex at nine as usual.

Inevitably, Alex was scowling and fidgeting when Charles strolled to his desk at one minute to nine, his nicotine levels boosted and a smile on his face. "I'm late for my next appointment," he complained.

"Hadn't you better go, then?" Charles said. "We can catch up later."

"No, I've been thinking outside the box," Alex said. "Alana's kicked David Saxton into touch and he's setting up a new company. The bank's raising funds for him."

"Aren't we working for Bishopstoke?" Charles asked.

"Nothing to stop us doing Saxton's corporate finance work as well," Alex smirked. "Double the money, double the fun. Saxton's going to need help with IT, and he likes you, doesn't he? We could second you for a fair fee."

"What might that fee be?" Charles asked.

Alex named a sum ten times his salary.

"I see," Charles said. "Well, you'd better ask him." He resolved to email Davey at once for a formal job offer. He couldn't wait to see the look on Alex's face when he resigned.

Chapter 46 Amy

To Amy's surprise, she discovered on her return to work that she'd hardly been missed. The merger with Bishopstoke was the talk of the office. No one spoke of anything else, as they speculated on what it meant for them: would they have an extra three days' annual leave like Bishopstoke staff, where would the merged company's offices be, and would the Veritable marketing team have jobs at all? All new products were on hold, and consequently so were the marketing campaigns. Parveen, with very little work to do, concentrated on honing her CV and encouraging her team to do the same. She took Amy to one side.

"I hope you'll come with me once I've secured a marketing position elsewhere in the City," Parveen said, her brown eyes earnest.

"Does that mean you rate my work?" Amy asked.

"Of course," Parveen replied. "I will admit my behaviour hasn't been perfect. You were foisted on me by David Saxton, and I resented that. But you've proved you can hold your own in a busy team."

"Thank you," Amy said, flattered. She considered whether to admit she didn't want to work for Parveen again, and decided honesty was the best policy. "I hope you don't mind, but I'm looking for a job outside financial services." She'd posted her CV on job boards, but Marty's offer was all she'd had so far. "Will you give me a reference?"

"An excellent one," Parveen assured her.

Within days, Parveen began to leave her desk for several hours at a time. Her absences were never explained. It was an open secret that she was having job interviews. She had just returned from one, and settled to filing her nails, when Amy said she was having lunch with her father and it might take some time.

They met at Rustica, taking a table outside so Charles could smoke. "Bottle of house white?" Charles ventured.

"Absolutely," Amy replied. She scanned the menu, looking for cheaper options. While Deirdre might have deep pockets, Charles had made it clear enough that he didn't.

"I've got news," Charles said, when the food was ordered and wine had been poured for them. "I'm moving to pastures new – in every sense."

"Splitting up with Deirdre?" Amy asked eagerly.

"That's part of it," Charles admitted. "I'm buying a flat so I can have my own space. In fact, it has two double bedrooms. You could live there too, if you like. I mean, it's got to be better than the broom cupboard you're renting right now."

As Amy was wondering what to say about Ross and her uneasy presence in his flat, Charles dashed any lingering hopes he'd return to Rachel. He added, "I love Deirdre and we're still a couple, but I shouldn't have moved in. If I don't put some distance between us, she'll be talking about marriage and babies. She's still young enough."

"Really?" Amy's jaw dropped.

"Oh yes," Charles said. "Dee's in her early forties, so it's possible. But I've been there, done that, already. I'm not the marrying kind." He drew on his cigarette.

Amy had a disturbing vision of Charles behind the wheel of his babe magnet Porsche, prowling the streets of London for women. She shuddered. If anything, she would prefer him to settle for married bliss and a new family with Deirdre. "Any more news?"

"I'm keeping the car if that's what you mean," he said, confirming her fears. "Actually, I'm changing jobs as well. Davey Saxton is establishing a new company and he's asked me to work for him. On extremely attractive terms, actually. It's all official now. I resigned from the bank this morning."

He must have seen he'd surprised her from the look on her face, for he added hastily, "That's confidential, of course. Only a few people know Davey Saxton's leaving Veritable after the merger. I just thought you might be one of them."

"Me?" Why should she be privy to sensitive information like that? "No, I had no idea. But Parveen's trying to swing redundancy packages for us."

"You wouldn't be entitled to one after just a year with Veritable, surely?" Charles said. "Also, you gave me the impression Parveen had horns and a tail."

Amy had reconsidered her opinion of Parveen somewhat. "She's okay, actually. Veritable put her under too much pressure before, that's all. She didn't have a big enough team or budget to meet their demands. And yes, she explained I wouldn't get statutory redundancy pay, but she'd do her best to squeeze an ex gratia sum out of HR. Apparently the City analysts ignore reorganisation costs when they look at our accounts, so Veritable can afford to be generous."

"They're certainly being generous to Davey."

"Anything they give me is a drop in the ocean then. A teaspoon of plonk compared with a crate of champagne. Anyway, why did you think I'd know?"

"I thought Ross might have told you."

She understood at last. "Is Ross going to work with you?"

"Yes, he is," Charles said. "He's a very clever young man. Davey holds him in the highest regard. I'm sure I will too."

Charles' opinion would change should he discover Ross merely considered her a friend with benefits. Of course, Charles still believed Ross was her boyfriend. He would hardly be persuaded otherwise once he knew she was living in Ross' flat. It was time to explain. "Do you want the good news or the bad news?" she asked.

"Oh, the good news, I should think." Charles looked expectant.

"I've moved into Ross' flat."

Charles was clearly delighted. "Congratulations. I take it you'll invite me round for supper soon?"

"Maybe." That would be an interesting evening. Ross could hardly turn away his new colleague. "However," Amy said, sorry to bring

Charles back to earth, "Ross isn't my boyfriend. In fact, he's going out with Kat, and she lives there too."

Charles looked stunned. "Kat? I thought her boyfriend was a gangster."

"It turned out Jeb wasn't her boyfriend, but he was a gangster. In fact, he tried to kill her."

"What's been going on?"

Amy took a deep breath. "It's a long story."

She was, thankfully, interrupted by the arrival of their food; several small plates of titbits and a half-baguette sliced and arranged on a square of slate.

"That doesn't look like enough," Charles observed. "Shall I order the same again?"

Amy giggled. "Yes, as you're getting a massive pay rise. Wasn't David Saxton annoyed when you dumped Deirdre?"

"I haven't dumped her, as you charmingly put it. In fact, Davey seems to think I'll move back in. Maybe I will. Anyway, you're not changing the subject that easily, young lady. Spill the beans."

"Kat disappeared," she began, "and Ross and I went to Birmingham to look for her."

"Why?"

"Well, it turns out that I'm the marrying kind," she said drily. "Kat stole my identity to wed an illegal immigrant for money." She told him nearly everything. It would have been too hurtful to describe her dalliance with Ross.

Even so, Charles was appalled. "You've packed as much into a week as I have in a lifetime," he said. "You shouldn't live with Ross and Kat after the way they've behaved towards you. It's a strange ménage à trois, and not in a good way."

Amy shrugged. "Kat's my friend. Ross has a beautiful flat, and his spare room is enormous." It was almost as swish as the Malmaison. Unlike the tiny converted cupboards in the basement, Ross' penthouse was spacious. He favoured cream throughout his flat, the only splodges

209

of colour coming from canvases by up and coming artists already selling for three times what he'd paid. Amy had a double bed, a walk-in wardrobe and a balcony. In practice, she had sole use of the bathroom too, as the master bedroom boasted an ensuite. Ross hadn't mentioned charging rent, and she wasn't planning to suggest it.

"Move into my spare room," Charles said. "It's close to the City, in Shoreditch. I'll ask my lawyers to hurry up with the purchase."

"No thanks," Amy said. Charles had said he wanted his own space. The last thing he needed was Amy playing gooseberry as he decided whether to return to Rachel, Deirdre, or anyone else. Of course it was preferable to Ross' luxurious flat, watching Ross and Kat canoodle, then dealing with the aftermath of the inevitable split. It was only a matter of time before Kat grasped how obnoxious Ross was.

"Actually," she said, "I could move to Birmingham."

Charles was puzzled. "Why would you do that? It's an even longer commute than Brockenhurst."

"Marty and Erik have offered me a job, as the marketing manager for their anti-cancer drug. It's good money, and interesting, but it's in the Midlands." She sighed. "I have until tomorrow to make up my mind. Marty phoned me today. I kept putting off the decision, and he's losing patience. He needs someone at once."

"Amy, you can't trust Kat as far as you can throw her. How can you even think about working for her brother?" Charles looked worried.

"Erik's not like Kat at all," Amy said. "He was prepared to die for her – and for me and Ross." Only luck, in the shape of a passing librarian, had saved Erik's life; indirectly, possibly Amy's too. Would the police have turned up in the tunnels otherwise? She would never know.

"It's a new venture," Charles pointed out reasonably. "How will you market a cure that isn't licensed yet? And they may call you a manager, but I doubt you'll have a soul working for you."

"It will be a marketing department of one," Amy admitted. "Initially, I'll be generating interest in the drug before it's released. It's sure to be a blockbuster. Don't you see? This could really build my career."

"Let me ask Davey if he can find you a role with us."

"I really don't want to work with Ross again," Amy said. "Don't forget, you just told me to move out of his penthouse."

Charles laughed. "You're right; I'm being dense. Where would you live if you moved to Birmingham? I don't know the city at all."

"I hardly know it myself," Amy admitted. "Erik lives in the Jewellery Quarter, and that's lovely, rather like Hatton Garden in London. Marty said I could take one of Erik's rooms rent-free, but I declined."

"Quite right," Charles agreed. "You'd both bring your work home then. There'd be no balance in your life any more."

She nodded, unwilling to remind him yet again about the unsocial hours she'd already worked at Veritable. In truth, she'd baulked because she didn't know if Marty was right about Erik. She suspected, in fact, that she liked Erik rather too much. After her foolish fling with Ross, Amy had resolved to let her next relationship develop slowly. "Marty's got another old workshop I can have, anyway. He assured me there were no cellars or secret tunnels." It was hardly stylish, he'd said, but he'd send one of his brood round to apply a lick of paint.

"You've convinced yourself, haven't you?" Charles said.

"I suppose I have," Amy said. If anything, Charles' scepticism had been a catalyst, crystallising her certainty. "At Veritable, I feel like a small cog in a big wheel running in a random direction. I'm excited to work with people I like and a product I believe in, where I can really make a difference."

Charles patted her hand. "That's exactly how I feel about working with Davey. Good luck, Amy. I guess you'd better let Marty know."

"I'll ring Erik too."

"I tell you what," Charles said, a glint in his eye, "Better still, why don't you just go to Birmingham to tell them, right now? I'd rather like to take the afternoon off. My boss can't stop me. I'll drive you there."

Amy grinned. "You just want a fast run on the motorway, don't you, Dad?"

"Dead right," Charles replied. "I'll take it to the ton. Well, what are we waiting for? My car's round the corner."

He wanted to meet Marty and Erik himself, she realised, as she followed Charles to his car. Her father was determined to make sure they were suitable employers. Would they mind? She thought not. Knowing Marty, he'd use Charles for some free IT advice.

Charles was bound to like her new bosses. Marty's cheeky charm was the ideal foil for Erik's honest intensity. With her marketing skills, they'd be a great team.

More than that, Amy knew she and Erik had faith in each other. One day, the trust between them might even become something more.